With unspoken assent, they headed back to the cabin. "I suppose you'll be needing this now."

Mary Anne dug the sketchbook out of her pocket. Her fingers brushed his as she placed it in Wallace's hands. Her touch sent a longing through him, a desire to walk hand in hand with her through the trees.

She cocked her head to one side, light playing on skin that had tanned under the summer sun.

The sketchbook dropped to the ground as he intertwined his fingers with hers and drew her close. He looked into her eyes, asking permission.

No stop sign appeared, only yield. Beneath the maple trees in the middle of the Vermont woods, he gently touched her lips with his, claiming them as his own.

She stepped back without speaking. She didn't have to. A shy smile lifted her lips, and a new light shone from those lobelia-blue eyes.

DARLENE FRANKLIN

Award-winning author and speaker Darlene Franklin lives near her son's family, including four precious grandchildren, in cowboy country—Oklahoma. Her daughter Jolene has preceded her into glory. Darlene loves music, reading a good romance and reality TV.

DARLENE FRANKLIN

Hidden Dreams

HEARTSONG
PRESENTS

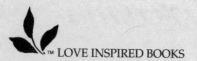 ™ LOVE INSPIRED BOOKS

ISBN-13: 978-0-373-48656-4

HIDDEN DREAMS

www.LoveInspiredBooks.com

Printed in U.S.A.

We have renounced the hidden things of dishonesty, not walking in craftiness, nor handling the word of God deceitfully; but by manifestation of the truth commending ourselves to every man's conscience in the sight of God.
—*2 Corinthians* 4:2

I wish to dedicate *Hidden Dreams*
to my beloved son, Jaran Franklin, who has met
the change in my circumstances with grace and love.
I couldn't have made it without you.

I also want to thank Mary Alward for her support.
I borrowed her grandmother's name
for one of my characters.

Chapter 1

Maple Notch, Vermont
March, 1927

Marabelle Lamont had never expected March to end the way it had after it started with such hope. If she didn't know better, she might think nature was playing some kind of early April Fools' prank.

The dark road ahead of her and the cup of coffee in her free hand reminded Marabelle of her present reality. The waitress at the restaurant in Burlington had gladly let her keep the cup. Marabelle had hated counting out change for the bill.

Dad had anticipated better days ahead when he bought the Victoria coupe two weeks ago. But using the car already sprinkled too many crumbs on the path she needed to hide. Pulling out a hundred-dollar bill would cement the memory. Only the changing letters of the town names gave any clue that she was making progress on her wild flight to Canada.

The hotel nestled next to the restaurant had tempted Marabelle—no, *not* Marabelle; she needed to use her birth name, boring old Mary Anne—to stop for a few hours. But registering for a room would require sensitive information, like identification and her signature. Awkward questions would be asked, such as why was a woman all alone asking for a hotel room when it was only a couple of hours past dawn?

As it was, she gained a few valuable tidbits of information while she forced herself to thoroughly chew each bite at the restaurant, as if she had all the time in the world. The breakfast was glorious—two slices of bacon served with fried eggs and pancakes covered with the marvelous syrup that made Vermont so famous. Most important, Marabelle learned she was near her goal of slipping over the border into Canada a few miles past St. Albans. Only one town lay between her and freedom: Maple Notch, Vermont.

Marabelle—*Mary Anne*—checked her appearance in the rearview mirror. Still pretty jazzy, even if she looked as pale and romantic as one of Valentino's sweethearts on the silver screen. She had tied a scarf over her bleached bob and worn her one remaining older dress since she had replaced most of her wardrobe with fancier clothing. She hoped that an ordinary Mary Anne wouldn't stand out, even if she was a young woman heading north to destinations unknown. If only the new car her father had bought her wouldn't garner attention…but she feared it did in this rural setting.

She set off once more, heading for Canada. To her right, in the increasing morning light, a bubbling stream winked between the trees. It was too bad she couldn't take the time to linger and enjoy the beauty around her.

She wished she could shed her identity as easily as she'd left the city. To do that she'd have to empty her suitcase of everything she owned. She wouldn't mind that, but with the border ahead, she'd need her documentation, so she couldn't lose herself so blithely. The farther she drove, the less traffic she saw. She hadn't passed a single car since her last stop. With God's favor, maybe she wouldn't until she had crossed the border.

This drive would be lovely in different circumstances. The beauty of the forest thrilled her, with the delicate greens of maples, oaks and birch, and the slightly darker green of new pine needles crowded against the bluish haze of spruce. Up ahead, tucked among the spring colors, she spotted a patch of red. *Not* a red maple tree, but one of the romantic covered bridges she had heard about.

The road swerved to the right and to the left, and then the entrance popped in front of her, much closer than she expected. Too late she saw the speed limit sign. *Ten* miles an hour? She was doing at least thirty. She hit the brakes as she entered the dark tunnel. Her front wheels gripped rickety boards and the bridge walls closed in on her car, like a clamshell on a hapless minnow.

The car skidded on the wooden decking, and she wrenched the wheel back to the center.

Wallace Tuttle tapped on his brakes for form's sake as he approached the old bridge. The drive from Grandpa Tuttle's farm to town provided welcome thinking time. With oncoming traffic so rare, he could practically drive it blindfolded. Tuttles had been going this way since before the Revolutionary War.

Nothing else moved along the road, but he always checked. He glanced at the shadowy entrance to the bridge and didn't spot any movement there, either. The bridge accommodated only a single lane of traffic but that rarely caused problems.

Seconds after he steered the truck into the darkened passage, a blue car barreled straight at him. He braked, the truck skidded and metal crashed into metal at the center of the bridge, bringing both vehicles to a halt.

His breathing stopped, then started again. He tapped one foot on the floor, then the other. Both legs were working. Loosening his grip on the steering wheel, he checked his chest, legs and arms. They appeared sore and bruised, but nothing was broken. *Praise the Lord.*

He stared toward the other vehicle, now diagonal across the twilit bridge. Squinting, he spotted a head slumped over the steering wheel. That car had been racing toward him at twice the speed of his vehicle. It was purely foolish to race onto a dark bridge without checking for oncoming traffic first. The other driver hadn't even turned on the headlights.

His truck door screeched as he opened it, and he stepped cautiously across the boards strewn with broken glass. His right knee caved a little, and he stumbled a bit, reaching for the nearest wall for support. This high-rolling stranger—it had to be a stranger, since no one in Maple Notch owned such a fancy car—would cost him time and money. The only other bridge over the Bumblebee River lay miles to the north.

He approached the other car with care. It was a marvel, the kind that screamed the sort of lifestyle that went with the driver's white-blond hair. Maybe she had drunk some of the illegal whiskey rumored to make its way through Chittenden County before taking the wheel.

She stirred, straightening slim shoulders and revealing a blood-streaked arm. Wide blue eyes opened for a second, grabbing his spirit with a soundless cry of fear and pain.

"Daddy." With that single word, she slumped against the door.

Chapter 2

The word tore at Wallace's heart. The surface sophistication suggested by dyed hair and deluxe vehicle hadn't protected the poor young woman. Rough skin showed beneath the torn silk of her dress.

He struggled to open the door, then reached for her wrist, noting her fast and erratic pulse. He ran quick hands over her exposed arm, finding only broken skin. Aside from a few scrapes here and there, only a bloody lump at the back of her head caused him major concern. He ran tentative fingers over the bump, and she moaned, jerking away from his touch. His pulse quickened.

"I'll go get you help." With a last gentle touch of her shoulder, he retraced his steps to his truck. The front tires had flattened, so he didn't bother getting into the cab. Should he leave her in the car or risk moving her to the bed of his truck? Leave her, he decided. The sooner he got to the farmhouse where he could call for help, the better.

He trotted down the road at a decent pace, although his muscles ached. He remembered how the stunned young woman had called for her father in her distress. For some reason, God had cast him in the role of Good Samaritan today. He would do his best.

A cool washcloth brushed over Mary Anne's forehead, tickling her to semi-wakefulness. She kept her eyes closed, trying to orient herself to her surroundings.

"I wonder who she is." She didn't recognize the man's voice.

"She didn't have any identification on her that I could find," said a woman this time.

Someone checking for identification…Mary Anne moved her lips but no sound came out.

"From New York, according to her car tags. Probably the city, from her accent." The second male speaker sounded vaguely familiar, like a radio personality never seen in person.

"She's one blessed lady for you to find her like you did." A large, callused hand probed her head, and she turned away at the pain caused by his touch.

The second man grunted. "If we hadn't 'met,' she wouldn't have been in an accident to start with."

Accident…car. Pain in her forehead kept Mary Anne from putting sense to the words. She felt an overwhelming sense of danger, a need for secrecy. Someone said she didn't have identification? *Good*.

She was lying in some stranger's house. She could feel crisp linen sheets and the weight of a quilt or coverlet covering her. The bed stretched out on either side of her, wide enough for a double bed. Odors unfamiliar to her, city girl that she was, of fresh grass, moist air and animals, wafted through a nearby window. A child's laughter, a dog's bark, the soft lowing of a cow greeted her ears.

Facts clicked into place. *Vermont. An old covered bridge. The accident.* That much came back to mind, and she groaned.

"She's coming around." The second man spoke. Bodies shuffled, and she felt a shadow pass between her and the window, then the warmth that must be the sun's returned.

Mary Anne forced her eyes open and squinted against the brightness of the noontime sun. A man with a black bag stood by her right side, a stethoscope draped around his neck. A slender, dark-haired woman stood across from him, dipping a washcloth into a water basin and replacing the one on Mary Anne's forehead. A younger man, with the same dark hair and good looks as the woman, hovered at the end of the bed. His muddied and torn jeans suggested he was her rescuer.

"Where am I?" Her words came out thick.

No one answered. "What do you remember?" The doctor tapped his chin with his finger.

Why wouldn't they answer such a simple question? "Where am I?" Even she could hear the panic in her voice.

"You're with friends." The woman wrung out the washcloth and placed a reassuring hand on Mary Anne's arm. "Let me go get you some tea."

The two men exchanged looks, a frown creasing the young man's brow.

The doctor said, "You have a nasty bump on your head. I'm going to ask you a few questions to help me determine the degree of injury you've received. So, do you know what day it is?"

"Wednesday? No. It must be Thursday."

"What year is it?" the doctor persisted.

"1927."

"And who's the president?"

Why was the doctor continuing with these silly questions?

"Herbert Hoover." She could almost hear her father saying "the dirty rat" and tears hovered behind her eyelids. She blinked them back.

The doctor nodded as if satisfied with her answers. Leaning forward to stare into her eyes with a scope, he asked, "What's the last thing you remember?"

Renewed danger signals warned Mary Anne to be careful of what she said, but the narrowed gaze from the man at the end of the bed suggested only the truth would do. "I was driving down the road and came across a covered bridge. And as soon as I turned onto the boards, a truck ran into me." *That's where I met him.* "That was you, wasn't it? Are you hurt?"

He shook his head. "No." He didn't sound very pleased about it. "Where were you heading?"

"Burlington." She said the first town that came to mind.

The frown returned to her interrogator's face. "You were heading in the opposition direction from Burlington."

"Oh, Wallie." The woman came back through the door, bearing a cup of steaming tea on a saucer. "Burlington's not that far away. I bet she just got lost up here in the woods." She held the china to Mary Anne's lips.

Mary Anne welcomed the sweet tea as an excuse not to say more.

"What is your name, dear?" The woman took a seat next to the bed. "Let me introduce myself first. I'm Clarinda Finch, and you're at my farm."

Mary Anne didn't miss the glare she sent the young man's way, daring him to comment on her introducing herself. Three pairs of eyes looked at Mary Anne, waiting for her to reciprocate with her name.

"I'm Mary Anne Laurents." The name came easily to her lips, even while her brain registered the lie. "And you're right, I did get turned around. If you'll just tell me where I can get my car, I'll be out of your hair."

The young man barked a laugh, and the doctor shook his head. "You're not going anywhere until we're certain what's going on with your head."

Am I your prisoner?

"Your car is stranded on the bridge, along with my truck." No wonder the man was frowning. "All the traffic for twenty miles around has to find another way across the river until we can get them towed."

Car? Towed? Without transportation, she couldn't leave even if she wanted to.

Clarinda made a shooing motion with her hands. "You two get out of here. Even without a medical degree, I can see Mary Anne needs rest and a bath, and I'm the one to help her with that. Thank you for coming when we called, Doctor. I will let you know if her condition changes. And Wallie, why don't you take care of getting a tow truck?" She followed the men to the door and shut it behind them.

Sitting beside Mary Anne, Clarinda patted her arm. "I feel I must apologize for my excuse of a brother. Anybody with half a brain could see you're worn out and scared to death."

At Clarinda's kind words, Mary Anne burst into tears.

"She's a beaut, ain't she?" Winnie Tuttle, Wallace's younger sister, whistled as she saw the coupe he was checking out for damage.

He nodded his appreciation for the car's elegance. "Not much call for fancy cars like this around here."

"I'd like to have a car like this someday." Winnie had jumped at the chance to help Wallace clean it after she returned from her ice skating practice. "Where do you think she's from?"

"New York. Maybe Brooklyn."

"These bags aren't fancy." Winnie struggled to lift a battered cardboard suitcase out of the trunk but managed to lay it gently on the floor.

"Not everything in New York is fancy." Wallace lifted the other suitcase, as heavy as his bags had been when he came home from college. He set it next to the first bag and studied the coupe. Painted as blue as the American flag, with a black roof, it was mighty handsome.

"But this car is fancy. I know. And you said she had that white hair." Winnie fingered her own dark locks, which she often complained of as ordinary.

Winnie was strong, a figure of earth and water, equally at home on a horse's back or on the ice. Not like the fragile beauty who remained abed, protected by Clarinda's strict warnings to leave her alone.

"We don't know anything about her, and no, you may *not* unpack her suitcases for her." The two of them trudged back to the house. "What you can do is help Clarinda fix supper. She's taken on nursing duties and is unlikely to leave Mary Anne's side long enough to fix us anything more than cold sandwiches for supper."

"And you think my cooking will be better?" Winnie laughed. "I'll rustle us up something, don't worry. You won't go hungry." She headed for the kitchen while Wallace tiptoed up to the spare room and placed the bags by the closed door.

Sighing, Wallace headed for the attic room which he had claimed as soon as he grew old enough to have one of his own. The tree outside the window had witnessed his flights when he'd attempted to escape from the house. Tear-soaked pages about his parents' deaths during the flu epidemic back in '18 filled the drawers of his desk. Some of his earliest sketches of local birds, encouraged by his membership in the Vermont Audubon Society, hung on the walls.

A fall-colored braided rug, made by his mother right before her death, held the pattern of two knees where he had spent hours in prayer after each huge event that had shaped his life. Feathered pillows he had poked and punched as he fell in and out of love during his youth lay on his bed, and awards from college hung on the walls.

The room and the farm were his life to this point.

But he'd met a girl fewer than four hours ago. Why did a single word she had whispered toss the fragments of his life on the floor and jumble everything in a game of Fruit Basket Upset?

Chapter 3

Every one of Mary Anne's muscles ached when she awakened, but a cushiony mattress helped relieve the pain. She couldn't remember how she acquired the injuries, nor who had taken her in for the night. She wasn't at home, she knew that much. Running her fingers through her hair, she found a lump at the crown of her head that set off alarm bells.

Her eyes flew open, and two facts registered. She was not in the house of any of her friends. She wasn't even in New York. *The accident.* An accident on a covered bridge had interrupted her flight plan, and the grumpy farmer had brought her to his sister's house. A local doctor had treated her, and they had taken her into their home. If only she could write a thank-you note like any good houseguest when she left.

Leave she must, as soon as possible. Fixing her car shouldn't take too long, since she was handy with machines. A turn or two with a screwdriver, a new tire if necessary, and she hoped to be ready to go.

First she had to get dressed. After all she'd endured yesterday, her hair must be a mess. Pulling at a few strands with her fingertips, she could tell someone had washed it. They hadn't stopped with her hair; she was clean from head to toe. Warmth crept into her cheeks at the thought. Clarinda, that was her name. She must have done it while Mary Anne slept.

As comfortable as the bed was, Mary Anne had to get going. Sitting up, she surveyed her surroundings. Two battered suitcases stood at the end of the bed. So someone had retrieved them from the car. Good. The dress she had on at the time of the accident hung clean and pressed on the wardrobe door. Even if her stockings hadn't survived the accident, she could slip her feet into her shoes without too much trouble. She wiggled her toes to make sure they could move. Bouncing her knees and waving her arms gave evidence that all four limbs still functioned.

Mary Anne's legs protested when she swung them to the side of the bed. The granny gown lifted above her knees, revealing a three-inch long scrape on one leg. The other leg featured cuts and nicks as well. Even silk stockings wouldn't hide the damage.

When at last she lifted her head, she found she was facing a mirror, and she gasped. Her pale face looked unhealthy and strange without makeup. Her almost-white bob, which had struck her as perfect in the hair salon, dulled in the morning light. Her overall impression was of sadness.

Her appearance matched her feelings. *Oh, Daddy.* Now he had died and left her alone—and terrified for her life.

Mary Anne lifted her chin. She missed her father and always would. But with the kind of money she had, she could start over, even here in the sticks, if she had a mind to. But keeping her options open required checking on her car. She set her right foot on the floor, followed by the left. As she stood, her legs wobbled and she pitched back against the bed.

"Whoa, there." A man's face bent over hers. His features revealed concern and an expression that said he didn't know what to do with her. After placing strong arms behind her back, he helped her under the covers. "Where did you think you were going?"

Wallace noted Mary Anne's grimace as she lay down. In his arms, she felt insubstantial, no heavier than a robin, and not much older than Winnie in spite of her flapper appearance. Beneath the bruises and the unnatural hair color lay a young beauty that wrenched his heart.

Wallace had promised himself an hour with a good book. That wouldn't happen, not with the patient awake. "Are you hungry?" As thin as she was, she could use a good meal or two.

"I am." She sounded surprised.

"Clarinda said she would fix you whatever you wanted. You only have to give the word."

"Biscuits and gravy." Her answer came out decisively. "I haven't had that in years."

"Biscuits *and gravy?*" Wallace repeated the words to be sure he heard her correctly.

"Oh, it's a Southern thing. My mother was from Alabama. I haven't had any since she passed." Sadness chased away the pain on her face. "Sausage gravy. Or you can make it from bacon or even ground beef, but sausage is best."

Some kind of white gravy, then. Clarinda could probably figure it out. "And how about some sausage and eggs to go with it?" Clarinda would pile her plate high, along with a mug of coffee and a tall glass of milk.

She nodded.

Wallace headed for the door but stopped. "You never did say where you were going."

"And you never told me your name." Laughing, she

straightened up against the headboard. "I want to check on my car, see if it's something I can fix."

The idea of this tiny city girl fixing a car was ridiculous. "It's been towed already. Waiting in the barn for me to get to it." He wouldn't work on hers until he finished repairs to his own truck. It needed headlights and one of the wheels not ruined in the accident had a suspicious leak in it.

Mary Anne shifted in the bed. "Your name?" The imperious tone of the question demanded an answer.

Wallace chastised himself. Of course she wanted to know his name. She was alone and defenseless in the home of total strangers. "I'm Wallace Tuttle. You're at the family farm, close to Maple Notch." Before she gave him another reason to linger, he slipped out of the room and trotted to the kitchen.

Clarinda wasn't there, but he soon found her in the garden, preparing for spring planting. As soon as she saw him, she stood and dusted off the knees of the men's overalls she wore when she worked outside. "Is she awake?"

"And asking for something called biscuits and gravy."

Clarinda nodded. "I've heard of that."

"She said her mother used to make it, before she died. A Southern dish, I gather."

"As young as she is, she already lost her mother? And you said she was calling for her father. It sounds like she's all alone. Poor thing."

Wallace wouldn't admit he had the same thought, wondering who had allowed her to drive so far alone. Was she running away from home? Did she have enemies? She was what storytellers might call a "damsel in distress," someone the Knights of the Round Table would ride to rescue.

The idea of himself as anybody's knight made Wallace chuckle. He was a farmer with glasses as well as a scholar with a pitchfork, two men within him who couldn't quite agree.

"Go back up there and keep her company until I bring her food. She must have a thousand questions. After breakfast, I'll help her get dressed and all."

A sigh followed a glance at the copy of *Walden* that Wallace held in his hand. He wouldn't get back to Thoreau's words today. Once Clarinda released him from his nurse-maid duties, he had to work on his book. Hurrying up the stairs to his room, he replaced Thoreau with a sketchpad. Then again, he could squeeze in a few minutes of reading time while his sister fixed breakfast. He settled in his chair for a few minutes of peace.

A short time later, after he picked up the tray Clarinda had prepared, he returned to the guestroom. Mary Anne was standing on two feet without shaking. She had managed to shove her feet into her shoes, impractical things that probably were all the rage back in New York. They looked as out of place with the nightgown as she did in the room.

"If Clarinda finds you up from bed, she'll fuss at both of us."

"You're back." She suddenly stopped and sat down on the bed.

"I'm under strict orders to keep you company until you get some breakfast." He rounded the bed. "Clarinda won't mind if you sit in the chair so you can sit at the writing table to eat."

Mary Anne glanced at her nightwear and, kicking off her shoes, drew her legs up and pushed her feet back under the covers. "I'll take my breakfast in bed, thank you."

Wallace almost chuckled at that. The dress she was wearing when she arrived exposed more of her than the neck-to-ankle nightgown. The fact that she still felt the need for modesty tickled him.

Unfolding a bath towel, Wallace prepared to spread it across her lap, but was that too intimate? Instead he handed it to her and waited until she had it smoothed over the quilt.

Setting the tray on her lap and picking up the book resting next to the plate, he sat down in his chair, glancing her way every once in a while.

Crunching bacon told him she had started to eat. "Mmm, something tastes different. Almost like—maple syrup?"

He shut the book as a lost cause. "Maybe so. It's cured over wood from maple trees." The bacon he ate at college always tasted different from the home-cured, but Mary Anne identified the reason. "It's tasty." He pointed to the biscuits smothered in white gravy, heavy with chunks of bacon and dotted with black pepper. "How does the gravy compare to what your mother used to fix?"

She split a biscuit with her fork and brought it to her mouth. As she slowly chewed, pleasure danced across her face. "Oh, this brings back memories. Here, you must try it."

When she handed him the fork like that, he couldn't refuse. The taste of the gravy lingered on his tongue for a few seconds, and he quickly swallowed the mouthful. "It's good. I'll ask Clarinda to fix me a plate."

Mary Anne tilted her head to one side and laughed. "I'm glad you like it." Winking at him, she made a display of savoring each bite. Clarinda would enjoy watching. Their guest had a sense of humor, a plus in her situation.

"When did your mother die?" The question popped out.

Mary Anne's skin paled even further. "I was only five. Daddy pretty much raised me on his own." She paused for a minute before continuing in a shaky voice. "He wouldn't let me cook, so I don't know how to fix many things."

Daddy...Did he dare bring up that subject? He would take the cowardly way out. "Is there someone you want us to contact, to let them know what has happened?"

"No." A shiver passed over Mary Anne, as if she was cold—or afraid.

She couldn't be cold, not on this mild early spring day and

under those covers. So, something—some*one*—frightened her. Once again he felt the need to rush to her rescue.

"I lost both of my parents, during the flu epidemic. First Dad, then Mom." Wallace fixed his gaze out the window, staring at the familiar farmyard, the place that had been his home and not his home for most of the past decade.

Mary Anne drew in a breath. "What did you do?"

"Our Aunt Flo took us in. The problem was, she runs a girls' school." He grinned at the memory. "At times, it was fun. There was quite a bit of competition for my attention, if you can imagine."

"And did anyone catch you?"

He smiled. "Lucky for me, no, they didn't. I dreamed of going away to college, and Aunt Flo made sure it happened. Clarinda married Howard and moved back out to the farm."

"And the girl I've seen running around the farm yard? Pretty thing, with dark hair in braids?"

"That's my little sister, Winnie. She likes living out here, where she is closer to the ice rink. She lives for skating."

The sad, fearful look left Mary Anne's face and she finished everything on her plate. Wallace stood and picked up her tray. "Can I get you anything else?"

Mary Anne shook her head. "I haven't eaten much breakfast for a while. If I keep up at this rate, I'll be too big for any of my clothes."

From what Wallace had seen, she could use a few more pounds on her frame. She didn't look strong enough to sweep the floor.

"If you still feel like getting up, I'll send Clarinda to help you get dressed."

At her nod, he left the room. When he dropped off the tray in the kitchen, he dipped a clean spoon into the gravy. He might ask Clarinda to make it again. In the afternoon, her husband, Howard, would take him into town to purchase parts for the truck. Until then, he would tramp to the old mill pond with his ever-present sketchbook. Once Winnie finished, he'd bring her home.

That was his plan, but his traitorous feet took him to the family grave plot, where his ancestors, from those who died shortly after the Revolutionary War to the most recent dead, his parents, were buried.

Sitting cross-legged on the ground, he looked at the simple inscriptions: Beloved wife and mother. Beloved husband and father. Would he ever find the same kind of love?

Chapter 4

On Saturday morning Mary Anne awakened from a dream about Daddy. It took a moment to remember her surroundings. She was at a farm near Maple Notch, the town lying between her and freedom—Canada. All that stopped her from leaving was a matter of fixing her car. That, and escaping Clarinda's ever-watchful eye.

Yesterday, Mary Anne admitted she wasn't in good enough shape to go anywhere. Last night she had stood and walked around the room, exercising her still sore muscles. Today she might make it, if she could get down the stairs without being discovered.

The girl, Winnie, said they had towed her car to the barn and then she had asked an endless stream of questions. When she wasn't asking about the car, she wanted to know about life in the city, and why Mary Anne had changed her hair color. Ten minutes in her company left Mary Anne exhausted, but she loved the chatter.

The sun cast pale light through the window. Mary Anne hadn't made it out of bed this early for months. Chuckling, she remembered the nights she hadn't made it to bed at all, until Daddy put his foot down. *Just because you've got money enough to burn doesn't mean you have to stay up all night. You can't burn the candle at both ends without getting consumed along with it.*

"Oh, Daddy." She'd hated his interfering ways, but now, how she wished she could have his advice. If only she could ask him one more question, have one more conversation, one last chance to tell him how much she loved him and missed him….

She dashed the tears away. *Stop wasting time and get moving. Put one foot in front of the other. A journey of a thousand miles starts with a single step.* Daddy had fought in Cuba before she was born, and he liked to talk about his travels.

The trip to Canada wouldn't cover a thousand miles, but she knew the first step: put on one of her clean dresses in the suitcase Wallace had brought to the room.

Swinging her legs over the side of the bed, she set her feet on the floor without wobbling. A good thing she had packed at least one pair of flats. High heels were out of the question until her body healed.

Mary Anne's right arm protested as she pulled the gown over her head. She forced herself to check her reflection in the mirror. Her face had largely healed, except for a patch of forehead covered by a bandage. She already knew about the lump at the back of her head. She had slept on her right side to keep from bumping it throughout the night.

Mary Anne sat down on the bed to gather her thoughts. Her bruises had largely faded; that wasn't the problem. But Maple Notch must be abuzz about the city girl who hadn't known better than to plow onto a covered bridge without taking any precautions.

Maybe staying as a guest of these kind people was the safest choice after all. All it had taken to transform herself from an ordinary girl to a flapper was money for new hair and clothes. If she stayed in Maple Notch long enough, her hair would return to its normal color and she could wear out-of-date fashions. She didn't know if she could ever change back to the girl she had once been, but she could try. Add sensible flat shoes and dirty fingernails, and she would have changed enough that no one would look at her twice.

As simply as that, the decision was made. Give her body time to heal and her hair time to grow. Her hosts wouldn't ask her to leave. Clarinda, and Wallie, too, in his own brusque way, had reassured her that she could stay as long as she wanted.

She would leave Maple Notch before Easter Sunday—Decoration Day at the latest. By then the gang chasing her would have given up hope of finding her.

"I can't get it to start." Wallace squatted and put his left hand on the engine crank for the farm truck. Half a crank, a full crank, but still the engine didn't start.

Mary Anne watched, frowning. He didn't want to blame her. The accident had caused more damage to her car than to his truck. The coupe's front bumper was scratched from side to side, and all four of the tires had shredded.

Without saying a word, she knelt beside him and motioned for him to drop his hand from the crank. Twisting just so, she laid her head against the grille and smiled as the first quivering rumblings of the engine made themselves known. The engine coughed, revved a few seconds, and Wallace wondered if this tiny dynamo might get it started after all.

Then it coughed, sputtered and stopped. Mary Anne tinkered with it a few more minutes, without success. She stood, her hand at the middle of her back. "We almost had it."

"There's a pretty good mechanic in town." Wallace rested one foot on the bumper, wondering how she had managed that much when he had failed. "He's closed for the rest of the day, but he can look at it tomorrow."

Mary Anne turned a bright smile in his direction and popped the hood open. "I'll take a look-see. Maybe I can figure out what is keeping the engine from turning over. It sounds like the alternator."

Wallace agreed, but he didn't have the know-how to fix it.

"At least it's not leaking oil." Mary Anne had already looked under the car. "That could be dangerous." Stretching on tiptoe, she bent over the engine and poked around. "It *is* the alternator, but I don't have any equipment to fix it. Maybe your mechanic friend can do that."

Alternator, bumper, tires—how much would the repairs cost? Mary Anne talked like money wasn't an issue. That didn't surprise him; anyone who could afford a Victoria coupe had money to spare. Enough money to tempt them into bad ways, Aunt Flo would have said.

His aunt worked hard to minimize any special treatment of students based on a family's financial status. Some of the girls with more money shared freely. Others hoarded every penny for themselves. Which kind would Mary Anne be? "Mary Anne" didn't sound like a rich girl's name. He had known a Mariam and a Mariel and several Maries. The only Mary Anne he had known was a distant cousin from his mother's side of the family.

By the time Wallace dragged his attention back to the Mary Anne in front of him, she had closed the hood of his truck and opened her coupe's hood instead. "Not much internal damage, from what I can see." Her voice echoed against the metal. She withdrew, not even the sweep of her almost-white hair able to hide the contentment on her face. "Although I do need to attend to an oil leak."

Closing the hood, she ran her hands over the spot where the truck had connected with her car. "Your truck is better off than my car, but I'm sorry about the damage." Sincerity glinted in her blue eyes. "The road was so deserted, I didn't give any thought to meeting another car on the bridge."

Wallace blew out his breath. Her irresponsible driving still irked him, but how could he stay angry when she apologized so prettily? "The important thing is that you are healing. Don't worry about my truck. I can take care of most of it myself." He couldn't believe he had allowed a woman to mess with his car.

A faint smile crossed Mary Anne's lips, as though she had read his mind. "Please let me do something to repay you for all the trouble I've put you through." Her eyes sought the floor momentarily, as if searching for something. "I would like to see the place where the accident happened."

Deep inside, Wallace debated the wisdom of her request. A lot of women he knew would shrink from driving into the same darkness that had ended so poorly the last time. But Mary Anne said that she wanted to see the bridge. "If you want to go right now, we can ride in the Model T." He nodded in the direction of the family car.

Scooting around the front to the passenger's side, she made sitting down an art form, as graceful as dance moves to music. He slid in beside her. "I haven't had a ride in an old Betty for a while." She patted the car at the use of a nickname. Throwing her head back on the seat, she leaned her arm on the right arm rest. "I've missed driving."

At that he laughed. "It's only two miles away. We could even walk." A part of him hoped she would agree.

Mary Anne's mind scrambled. How far was two miles? In the city, they counted distance in terms of blocks. She had heard somewhere that twelve blocks equaled one mile, but back in New York, the length of the blocks differed whether they were headed north and south or east and west.

Two of anything shouldn't be all that far. They were unlikely to run into strangers, and she had sensible flats on her feet. "Let's do it."

"Are you sure?" Without waiting for an answer, he opened the door and swung his legs out.

"Yes. Let me get my coat, though."

Wallie walked with her to the house and up the stairs.

"I don't need a chaperone."

He grinned. "My room is in the attic. As long as we're going out, I'm going to grab my book."

Mary Anne scratched her head. He couldn't walk and read at the same time, could he? The image of a man with his nose buried in a book, maneuvering his way up and over curbs and through foot traffic on busy city blocks tickled her sense of the absurd. She had seen a few people like that, tourists too busy reading a travel guide to actually enjoy the visit. Wallie was no tourist, so she wondered what book he would bring.

She removed her coat from the wardrobe and stared at the boots sitting in the corner. From her window she had glimpsed a few patches of snow. They could encounter snow or mud, or both, so she exchanged her flats for her boots. The thought of a good walk raised her spirits. Since she'd bought her car back in New York, she hadn't walked anywhere.

Wallie had changed into a warm jacket as well, a notebook peeking out of a large side pocket. He glanced at her boots. "Good choice. And I brought you this. It might get cold out there." He handed her a red knit hat.

The head covering reminded her of a favorite hat and scarf set from her childhood. She skipped down the stairs ahead of him, eager to get under the open sky and fresh air.

They paused by the kitchen on the way out. "We're going to the bridge, but we'll be back before meal time."

He grabbed a canteen and filled it with water. "In case we work up a thirst." His whistle pierced the air. The walk gave Mary Anne her first opportunity to see beyond the farmyard. A fence surrounded a good-size plot, resembling the victory gardens that had sprung up around her neighborhood during the Great War. She had enjoyed working with the women of the neighborhood, digging in the dirt. Maybe she could do the same thing here if she stayed long enough.

What was she thinking? She needed to leave Maple Notch as soon as possible. If she stayed long enough to plant a garden, she might want to stay until harvest. Even if Canada wasn't her goal, no one, no matter how generous their hospitality, wanted a guest to move in permanently.

Past the yard, they walked beside a rough-hewn fence that looked as weathered as the barn. She ran her hand along the top rail, feeling the knobs and knots. Fields lay to the right and left of the road, extending into the distance. Did the Tuttles own all of this land? She couldn't imagine it. "Does all this belong to your family?"

"I'm afraid it does." Wallie's laughter sounded a bit rueful. "Tuttles have lived here through good times and bad since before the Revolutionary War." He shoved his hands into his pockets. "Up ahead, near where the bridge crosses the river, one of my ancestors lived in a cave and kept on farming the land by night, to keep it safe from Tory opposition." He flashed a grin at her. "Unfortunately, her beau's father was a Tory."

"But they got together in the end?"

"Yes."

"And they lived happily ever after?" she teased. The way Wallie told the story suggested the couple had made a go of it.

"Yes, but then their son almost lost the land during the Year of No Summer."

"The what?"

"People around here call 1816 the Year of No Summer. Every single month there was a killing frost and sometimes even snow. He owed money to the bank, so he needed a good crop that year. He figured a way to make his crops grow in spite of the frost. He burned out the stumps, and it kept the ground warm." Another grin lifted his face. "And along the way he fell in love with the banker's daughter."

That brought a chuckle from Mary Anne. "So your family has been farming here for over a hundred fifty years."

"Not exactly." Wallie shrugged. "My grandmother was a teacher. She opened a female seminary in Maple Notch, and my grandfather was the town constable. But then my father moved back out to the farm and started growing crops again."

"So who took over after he died?"

The carefree joy disappeared from Wallie's face before he forced another smile. "Howard married Clarinda about that time. They came out to the farm. I stayed out here during the summers, and at the school during the school year."

He pointed to a fenced-in area a little higher than the field. "There's the cemetery up ahead. I often stop to visit when I'm on foot."

"Let's go, then." Mary Anne found the trail leading from the road and took off without waiting for an answer.

Wallie trotted to catch up with her.

A moment later, he had stopped moving, and she walked back. While he stood as straight as a board and quiet as a tree, his hand flew over a page in his notebook. His pencil filled the page with the wing.... foot....beak...of a goose. This Vermont farmer was an *artist?*

Not wanting to disturb his concentration, she watched without speaking, fascinated as his fingers added the grass and plant of the nest peeking out beneath the downy underbelly of the goose. He shaded in two eggs.

Mary Anne had seen kittens born but never newborn birds.

The baby sparrows and robins she had spotted were on the verge of flying and independence.

Standing on tiptoe, hoping to catch sight of the sitting mother for herself, Mary Anne stumbled a bit, disturbing the peace. Another goose ran at them, wings spread, hissing like a snake. Scared, she jumped back.

"That's our cue. He wants us to leave his family alone." Wallie flicked his wrist to check his watch. "If we're going to make it to the bridge and back by suppertime, we'd best be on our way."

Mary Anne threw a last glance over her shoulder, still entranced by the pair of geese. Perhaps another time she could beg Clarinda for stale bread or biscuits and return. In the city people were warned against feeding ducks, but she had seen another little girl feeding a duck and wanted to share that experience. Now was her opportunity. Maybe she'd even get to watch the goslings grow.

With a final glance, she trotted after Wallie. Her boots splashed through mud and other unpleasant things underfoot. He waited for her at the end of the lane, elbow leaning on the fence rail as if he had been there all day. He grinned at her approach. "What took you so long?"

She pretended to take him seriously, walking past him, headed toward the bridge. "I stopped to look at the geese. What are you waiting for, Wallie?"

He caught up with her in one long stride. "Call me Wallace, please. Wallie is a childish nickname."

That drew laughter from Mary Anne. Strange, how "Mary Anne" felt like a nickname since she had been calling herself "Marabelle" for the past year. "Wallace." She drew the name out, trying it on her tongue. Both names suited the man beside her, part farmer, part student. "Those sketches you were drawing of the birds were good." Her attempts at art resembled stick figures, unless sewing counted. She had embroidered a few things that hung in the apartment that had been her home with Daddy.

Things she had left behind, along with almost everything else she had ever owned. Maybe here in the Maple Notch of Wallace's drawings, a place vibrant with life and peace, she would find a better home.

Maybe if she stayed here long enough, she'd even find life and peace for her own.

Chapter 5

Mary Anne liked his drawing. The only other people to say so were his family, except his brother-in-law who tended to snort at such foolishness. An editor had paid Wallace an advance so he could complete the project, with drawings and text, about the native wildlife and plants of northern Vermont. That interest drove Wallace into the fields and woods at every opportunity.

Until now, he had never let a stranger, except the editor, see his strange hobby, and Mary Anne liked it.

"Thank you." His voice sounded as light as his heart, and his feet sped him forward to the old bridge, the courting bridge, or the kissing bridge, as the people of the town called it. What would Mary Anne think of the planks in the wall that broadcast a couple's intentions to wed?

As light as his feet were dancing, Wallace could have closed the distance to the bridge in a short time. But Mary Anne lingered so long that they might have to turn back before ever reaching their destination. "It's so pretty here." She swept the horizon with waving arms.

"You should see it in the fall." Maybe she would. Or would she be like the geese, heading south before winter struck in its fury?

With every bump and rock on the road familiar to him, Wallace knew when they neared their destination. "I see it!" Mary Anne splashed ahead, heedless of the puddles, and Wallace sprinted to keep up with her.

"Is that a cave I see down there?" She halted at the entrance to the bridge, studying the river bank as if delaying her stepping on the boards.

"Yes." Another time he might show her the cave and tell her more of his family's history.

The sunshine cast Mary Anne's figure into a dark shadow on the floorboards. She poked her head in cautiously. "Is it safe for pedestrians? What if a car heads this way?"

"They can squeeze by if you cling to the wall." Wallace meant to be funny, but the terror on her face testified to his failure. "Yes, we're safe. In the unlikely event a car heads this way, we can retreat to the trusses. Plenty of room."

Moving one cautious foot in front of the other, she walked forward as if trying to drink in the bridge with all five senses. In the dim interior of the bridge, with only an occasional strip of light where the roof boards had separated, she wouldn't be able see well. The smells of a century of history had burrowed themselves into the structure. Wood, horses and even gasoline were part of the mixture now.

Their boots made soft noises while they crossed the span. As they approached the center, he touched her arm. "Stop. There's something I want to show you."

She allowed him to lead her to the side. "Reach up and touch the wall right here." He indicated the plank in question.

Standing on tiptoe, she found the same spot and tilted her

head back to study it. "There's something written there but I can't tell what it says."

"Carved initials. They've been up there so long that they're almost invisible. But I can tell you what they say."

"This is where I'm supposed to ask, 'What do they say?'"

From Wallace's limited experience with girls, they loved the story. "They're the very first initials carved on the board. Back before there even was a bridge across the Bumblebee. They say J.T. and S.R."

"J.T.—as in Tuttle?"

Wallace grinned. "My grandfather's grandfather. When old Josiah proposed to Sally Reid during the middle of the Revolutionary War, he carved their initials on a tree. Then that tree ended up as part of the bridge."

"How sweet." Mary Anne ran her hands over the board, exploring the other carvings. "There must be dozens of them carved up here now."

"Hundreds, more like." Wallace pointed to a different plank with more recent carvings. "That's my parents—1900."

Squinting, she studied the wall. "The turn of the century."

He nodded. "A new century was a good time to start a new life together, that's what Ma used to say." He added words he had never used before. "Someday I hope to add my initials to the bridge."

She reached out and squeezed his hand, and Wallace's dream expanded to fill every nook and cranny of his heart.

"Wallie? Is that you?"

The magic of the carved initials faded to its proper place, and Mary Anne dropped Wallace's hand at the sound of Winnie's voice. Boys and girls in New York did the same kind of thing, scratching their names on poles, bricks and painted walls.

Not that she would ever carve her initials into anything.

A good thing Winnie showed up when she did, before Mary Anne's impulsive action suggested something to Wallace other than gratitude and even, perhaps, friendship.

Winnie trotted to the center of the bridge, two dark braids bouncing against her coat. "You're showing her the Kissing Wall."

Heat flooded Mary Anne's face at that observation, and she thought she saw color on Wallace's cheeks.

Winnie didn't react to their discomfort. Flinging herself against the wall, she threw her arms high overhead. "And here stands Winifred Tuttle, the Junior National Skating champion." She pirouetted and glided across the floor to the center, where she brought her hands over her head and posed.

"You're heading for the mill again." Wallace's mouth quirked into an expression between a scowl and a smile.

"Of course! How else will I ever be a national champion like Frank Sawtelle?"

Ice skates hung over Winnie's left shoulder, and Mary Anne remembered how much Wallace said she enjoying skating. Frank Sawtelle must be her idol.

"Come on ahead. We're heading back to the house anyhow."

"Okay." Twisting and turning like she was on the ice, Winnie whistled a tune.

Mary Anne's head bobbed in time to the music. "'When the red robin comes bob, bob, bobbin' along.'" She finished the song, singing the lyrics made famous by Al Jolson. Winnie turned and glided and flew backward in a series of movements that she probably had rehearsed on the ice countless times.

When they reached the end of the song, Winnie bowed, and Wallace clapped. A moment later they exited the bridge to bright sunshine. The tree branches strained toward the sky in search of life-giving sunshine. Winnie turned left, on a road Mary Anne hadn't noticed before, and waved goodbye. "It was good to see you again, Miss Laurents! Sometime I'll have to play my Al Jolson recordings for you."

"I'll look forward to that."

Winnie trotted down the road.

"You keep doing the most surprising things." Wallace's smile took the sting out of the way he shook his head. "Clarinda doesn't quite approve of Jolson. When I first heard his music in college, I thought the angels in heaven couldn't sing much prettier."

Mary Anne didn't know what surprised her more: the fact that Wallace liked Al Jolson, or that he had attended college. His liking the jazz musician was the great surprise, she decided. Everything about him, except for the farmer's overalls, screamed student. "Where did you go to college?"

"The University of Vermont. Did you know it's the fifth oldest college in all of New England, after Harvard, Yale, Dartmouth and Brown?" He waved her stuttering response away. "Very few people outside of Vermont know that, but we're quite proud of the fact in this part of the world."

Now that the sun was dropping low in the sky, the temperature had fallen with it. Mary Anne tugged the collar of her coat about her neck. She'd had quite enough of college boys in recent days, with most of them too eager to teach her things she didn't want to know. No wonder Daddy had warned her against the lot of them.

What would Daddy say about the man next to her? College graduate he might be, but she couldn't imagine him enticing a girl into a speakeasy and then taking advantage of her.

One bad decision had followed another on that terrible night. Would it haunt her forever?

Wallace had encountered his share of flappers. Even the most studious of the co-eds followed the fashions of the times.

A few of them embraced the lifestyle as well. Someone was operating a speakeasy here in Maple Notch, and he had heard rumors of moonshiners. His grandfather, the town constable, would have brought that to a quick end. But Grandpa had fought his war, losing his arm during the Civil War, and Wallace must face his. He would fight with words and laws, and hope he never had to go to battle with guns. For the most part, the revelers went one way, and Wallace went his.

In spite of her strange hair color and shiny new car, Mary Anne didn't resemble the flappers he had met. Whether her fearful flight stemmed from innocence or guilt, she had disrupted his peaceful life. Since their first encounter, he couldn't stop thinking about her.

The fact that she liked his drawings pleased him more than it should. If Wallace spent much time around her, he wouldn't finish writing the book by the editor's deadline in mid-October. After supper, he would head to the abandoned cabin where his great-grandparents had once lived. He had food, firewood, paper and pen, everything he needed to get to work.

Wallace's hopes for a quick escape disappeared when Winnie arrived at the farmhouse in time for a late dinner. He hadn't accounted for his sister's propensity for telling a good story.

"Yep, I caught them standing on the Courting Bridge, under the Kissing Wall." Winnie rolled her eyes. "They were *holding hands.*"

Howard Jr. and Arthur, Clarinda's two boys, guffawed.

"They were, were they?" Clarinda's eyes twinkled, and Wallace wanted to groan. His older sister had quizzed him at every opportunity about the girls he met at college. She probably thought God had brought Mary Anne to the farm for a romantic purpose.

Mary Anne's cheeks had turned a gentle pink, but she

stayed calm. "He was telling me some of your family's stories. All I know about my grandparents is that they were among the first people through Ellis Island." Her eyes flared slightly, as if she revealed an embarrassing detail. "It must be wonderful to have a family history as old as America herself."

Wallace took his family's heritage for granted. The Tuttles were one of a handful of original Maple Notch families, along with his distant cousins, the Reids.

"I think people who leave the only home they've known to come to America must be terribly brave. When they don't even know the language..." Clarinda shook her head. "I speak a little French. *Parlez-vous français*, Mademoiselle Laurents?"

Pure confusion flooded Mary Anne's face. "Uh...I guess not."

Clarinda lifted her shoulders in a delicate shrug. "I've heard some people speak only English after they arrive, wanting to blend in with the melting pot that is America. But I think it's a pity, myself. Not many people here speak two languages well. Even after four years of studying French at the seminary, I doubt I could survive in France without a translator by my elbow."

After that, conversation turned to other channels. Wallace left early, promising to return Winnie to Aunt Flo before retiring to his cabin. Upon his return from town, he pulled Howard's car into the yard and grabbed his things from the backseat, heading for the old cabin at a brisk walk.

The old Reid cabin was the perfect place for him to sharpen his focus on his goal, to shut their unexpected guest out of his mind.

Chapter 6

On Friday morning, Mary Anne imitated Clarinda through each step of making biscuits from scratch. After Mama's death, Daddy did all the cooking, but he lacked the patience to teach her. He took over laundry as well, and all the other tasks women usually did, without a complaint. Tears stung her eyes.

"Something's troubling you." Instead of rolling the biscuits out, Clarinda patted them flat with her floured hands. "I've got a good ear for listening, if you want to talk about it." She handed a glass to Mary Anne after showing her how to cut biscuits with the rim of an inverted tumbler.

How Mary Anne wished she could unburden her heart to this kindhearted lady. But talking about Daddy's death would involve explaining about the money and the trouble it had caused. That part was best kept secret. "I've got some things on my mind, that's all."

Clarinda made cutting out the biscuits seem effortless,

but the ones Mary Anne cut clung to the edges. "What do I do with the leftover dough?"

"Roll it back into a ball and pat it flat again. You try it."

Mary Anne coated her hands with flour but she couldn't get the dough flat. One of the biscuits looked like a right angle, rising from the seashore to the mountains. As long as she was making a mess of things, she plunged ahead, rolling the leftover dough into a single semi-round shape.

Clarinda studied the biscuits. She tapped the recipe card Mary Anne hadn't looked at once against the countertop. "The recipes for shortcake and coffee cake, almost anything made with flour, are a lot like this, with some variation in the amount of butter and sugar and such. Other things require eggs. You'll get the hang of it." She slid the sheet with the biscuits into the oven. "Next time I'll let you make the biscuits by yourself. Anyone who loves biscuits and gravy the way you do needs to know how to make it for herself."

"Do you always make so much?" Mary Anne gawked at the number of eggs Clarinda broke into her mixing bowl. After ten, she lost count.

"Sometimes more, when Wallace is eating with us."

Wallace hadn't returned, then. A cloud slid across the sun, blocking the sunshine from the window. She felt his absence more than she expected.

"He's over at the cabin, working on his book."

His *book?* He had left the house for several days to read?

Clarinda laughed. "He must not have told you about his pet project. A publisher is interested in the book he's writing about the animals and birds in northern Vermont."

The sketch Mary Anne had seen Wallace draw must be part of this project. "I can't imagine writing a whole book." Or wanting to write one.

"He takes it very seriously. He says no one has done a proper study on the subject, and if we're not careful, we may end up losing animals we take for granted. The way the hunters killed almost all the buffalo and the passenger pigeons have all died."

Worry about animals dying seemed unimportant compared to the tenements in New York, but maybe farmers never knew the sting of hunger. "That's interesting."

Clarinda laughed. "You sound like Howard. He thinks now that Wallace's finished school, he should either get a proper job or settle down on the farm."

An ordinary job would never satisfy the man who took the time to watch a pair of geese and reproduce them with such precision. Mary Anne could see that. "Is it for grown-ups?"

Clarinda shrugged. "Yes, but Wallace has a way of putting things into words everyone can understand. You don't have to be a university professor to read it." After a glance at the clock, she slipped on an oven mitt and brought out the biscuits. They lacked the uniform color of Clarinda's biscuits, ranging from almost burnt to barely done.

While the biscuits had baked, Clarinda had whipped together the rest of breakfast, and now Howie and Arthur tumbled in, followed close on their heels by a cute tot with blond curls. The boys had dragged on blue jeans and shirts, and were ready for school.

Arthur turned over a biscuit with an almost black bottom, but he just slathered extra butter on it. This breakfast proved no exception to the always lively meals, although Mary Anne found herself listening for Wallace's quiet chuckle, his banter with his nephews, his light teasing of both little Betty and Winnie.

Without his presence, the meal tasted a little bland. Clarinda offered to take Mary Anne into town or to go shopping for her. But the only things Mary Anne needed were car parts she wanted to choose for herself, and she wanted to avoid people until her bruises had faded.

"I usually spend Fridays in town, but I don't like leaving you on your own. Are you sure you don't want to come?" Clarinda repeated her earlier question.

Mary Anne shook her head.

"I will see you this afternoon, then, after the boys and Winnie are out of school. Take whatever you want for food." She reminded Mary Anne of all the items in the ice box and pantry, as if she hadn't already explained the system to her guest.

"I'll be fine." Mary Anne was looking forward to time alone. After a lifetime living in a crowded apartment, she craved time to plan, time to grieve, time to simply be. Here, if someone didn't check on her at least once an hour, they seemed to feel they had neglected her.

And Wallace has been gone since Tuesday. Mary Anne looked out the window, wishing she'd had the courage to ask Clarinda where the old cabin might be. But she couldn't ask that, not without revealing too much about herself.

Wallace cut up potatoes and onions while his bacon fried in the pan. He added potatoes, cooked them to a perfect crispness, finished off the meal and cleaned the dishes. Now he would fill a giant mug with coffee and write down what he had observed that morning.

Wallace's habit of delaying breakfast would shock Clarinda if she ever found out. Dawn and dusk drew animals to the Bumblebee River like a bee to nectar. He loved watching the doe teach her almost-grown fawn the wisdom of the forest, or any one of the other animals bringing their young out.

This morning a family of raccoons had caught his eye. Betty had broken a string of beads, and he dropped a few of the colorful orbs on the ground to see what the babies would do. From his post, he watched as first one curious nose, then another, approached the bright beads. When they reached for one with their paws, it rolled away, and they chased it until they finally grasped it.

The mama raccoon kept watch. She sensed Wallace's presence—she sent a furtive glance in his direction—but she didn't warn the young ones away. The fact that she trusted him with her babies made him strangely pleased. After they finished their play and presented their gifts to their mother, the family escaped into the growing sunshine, their treasure safe in their possession. He jotted notes next to the sketches he had made.

Did the color of the beads matter? The family cat, a girl, preferred pink to any other color. Maybe there was a reason girls liked pink. Mary Anne would look pretty in pink.

He drew his mind back from dangerous waters. Raccoons were in no danger of extinction, so he should focus on different animals. He thought he had spotted a spiny soft-shell turtle once, and even cottontail rabbits didn't appear as often as they used to. He'd love to catch sight of a silver-haired bat; he should set up watch in the cave where the Reids had lived during the Revolutionary War.

Entranced by the raccoons, Wallace had lingered at the river longer than usual, and he was hungry. After he finished his belated breakfast, he sat on the front step to the cabin, leafing through the sketches of the baby raccoons at play. He wouldn't mind spending an entire year following the little ones from birth to maturity. These woods held the possibilities for more books than a man could write in a hundred lifetimes. His problem was settling down to one.

Today his pencil danced across the pages as he detailed the account of the baby raccoons. Maybe he could coax more beads from Clarinda another time, or maybe gather coins and beads and buttons. Study which attracted more attention.

Out here, in a cabin set far enough back from the road that no one bothered him unless they came on purpose, he regained a sense of what the world might have been like after creation.

Free of sin and worry, and full of faith and joy and peace. The way God meant life to be.

Mary Anne counted the money in her suitcase. Even though she hadn't dared to go to the bank to withdraw everything in her account, she had kept a large sum in her house. She had plenty to live on until she got settled somewhere. *Thank You, God.* Among other things, she wanted to give something to her hosts without raising their suspicions.

Of more immediate concern was what to wear around the farm. In a fit of generosity, Mary Anne had given away her old wardrobe as she purchased new clothes. The only dress she had held back was her favorite, one of her mother's dresses. If only for sentimental reasons, she didn't want to let it go.

None of her new dresses suited life on the farm, although she hoped they would be suitable for life in Quebec City or Toronto or Montreal. The larger Canadian cities probably followed the same fashion trends as New York.

Thinking of Quebec City or Montreal, Mary Anne realized she had been foolish to think she could stop as soon as she arrived in French-speaking Canada. It took only one single question, *"Parlez-vous français?"* to uncover her lack of knowledge of the language. They spoke English in Toronto, didn't they? If only she could read a map to figure out how to get there from here.

Life on the farm hovered between the practical and the joyful. No one would call Clarinda's dresses boring, but their splash came from color rather than cut. She hadn't commented on the clothes she found in Mary Anne's suitcase. Instead she had quietly added a few other dresses more suitable to daily life on a farm. Mary Anne was wearing one today.

She wandered down the stairs and out to the living room. The bookcases drew her, and the privacy allowed her to explore to her heart's content. They looked like the family that owned them, solid, with roots extending back for over a century, some worn, some shiny and new. She ran her hands over the bindings, treasuring the feel of the rough cloth of some and the smooth leather of others. Toward the bottom of the shelf, she discovered a cache of children's picture books, obviously well-loved. She picked out one at random. The figures on the pages reminded her of stuffed animals: a teddy bear, a donkey, even a little pink pig. Maybe she could ask one of the boys to read it to her when they got home from school.

Clarinda ran the household like a chauffeur treated his car, keeping it well oiled, shiny, in the best condition. Nevertheless, Mary Anne decided to run a feather duster along the bookshelves and over the tables in the living room, gathering up the pillows to plump them into softness. A tortoise-shell cat followed her, batting at the feathers with her claws. After finishing, Mary Anne sat on the couch and ran the duster in circles around the floor, encouraging the cat to play. She chased and pounced and dragged the duster out of Mary Anne's hand. Scattering feathers across the floor, she ran in the opposite direction with a single prize feather in her mouth.

Chapter 7

Mary Anne stared at the swishing tail of the departing cat. Gathering the fallen feathers, she dropped them into the trash basket. So far her efforts at "helping" had resulted in burned biscuits and a ruined feather duster. Housework, two, Mary Anne, none.

Every day she stayed at the farm, she cost her hosts money, from the doctor's bill to the repairs to Wallace's truck. If only she felt well enough to fix it for him. But why should he trust her with his truck? Girls weren't supposed to know how machines worked.

Mary Anne decided to eat lunch early. Cream waited to be churned into butter, but she didn't dare try it. Grabbing a hard-boiled egg, she headed outdoors. She and Wallace had never made it to the family cemetery the other day, after watching the geese on their nest. If she started now, she could get there and back before Clarinda returned with the children.

The road looked remarkably similar, whether heading to

the right or left, but she felt certain they had turned left when they headed for the bridge. After topping off her canteen from the pump in the yard, she headed left. Empty fields on one side balanced the crowded forest on the other. She wished she had Wallace's gift for putting pictures on paper. She'd love to capture this view with her pencil. The best she could do would be to take leaves back with her and run a crayon over the ridges to get their outlines. Maybe she'd come back with the children and do that sometime.

Caught up in her study of the trees, she almost missed the turn for the cemetery. Only an overgrown path suggested that humans passed this way. A short distance after the geese's nest, she found a plot with perhaps fifty grave markers.

Even this early in the spring, when grass didn't require cutting, someone took care of the cemetery. Fresh flowers grew around each grave, from the tiniest to the few graves with granite gravestones. Crosses that the years had pounded close to the ground marked a handful. Others had words scratched into the wood, and later ones had words and pictures carved in granite. Whether plain or fancy, each memorial represented someone loved and grieved.

Oh, Daddy. Before she had left New York, she had met with her pastor in secret to give money so that Daddy would receive a proper burial. If the day ever came that she could return to the city, she would find his grave and make sure someone took care of it. Daddy didn't have anyone else who would care.

Wallace didn't know how lucky he was. The middle of the cemetery held her tears for the lives the place represented and the one person she missed more than anybody in the world. Her tears turned to song, her surest cure for sadness ever since her childhood. "Amazing Grace," "Blessed Assurance," "Fairest Lord Jesus"—she had memorized every verse.

Various scents pushed their way into her consciousness, the smells of new grass and flowers pushing their way through wet dirt. Mixed with the earthy fragrance smells she sensed a sharper aroma, that of burning wood. Looking around, she located a single column of telltale smoke not far in the distance.

Wallace's cabin.

Wallace sank deep into the atmosphere surrounding his retreat. He couldn't describe it as quiet. Here and there mice skittered across the ground and birds flapped their wings overhead or sat in the trees and sang their mating calls. Once or twice he had brought his cat out to the cabin with him, but in general he preferred the cabin to remain the way it was when his great-greats first moved to Maple Notch. Closing his journal, he let the peace of the day flood him.

An unexpected sound intruded on his solitude. A woman's voice sang "Fairest Lord Jesus."

"'Fair are the meadows, fairer still the woodlands, robed in the blooming garb of spring.'"

The hymn captured his feelings for the day. He joined in the song. "'Jesus is fairer, Jesus is purer.'"

"'Who makes the woeful heart to sing.'" Alone, Mary Anne's voice rose in a final measure. "Aaaa—men."

The angels couldn't have sounded much better when God created the earth. Mary Anne's voice was so beautiful, for a moment he forgot he was irritated with her for interrupting his peace.

"What a beautiful day." Mary Anne twirled in a circle. "I'm glad I decided to come out this way."

She looked around as if seeking a place to sit, and Wallace scooted over on the step, making room for her. Gathering her skirts around her legs, she sat down and smoothed out the wrinkles in the skirt. The sun had warmed the air somewhat, or perhaps she had become heated on her walk, and she unbuttoned the front of her coat. The sailor collar peeking out took some of the harshness away from her bobbed hair and pale face.

"Your journal." The words came out with a reverential air. She put her hand on his shoulder and leaned in, as if unaware of the effect she could have on a man. She remained as forward as any flapper he had ever met, while she reflected an inborn innocence. "Raccoons! Do they live near here?"

"They come down to the river. All the animals do, at dawn and at dusk. Only the brave come in the middle of the day, when predators abound."

Her laughter had a mocking tone. "Like the people who go to speakeasies from dusk to dawn and spend their days abed. I've always been more of a morning person."

She leaned over further, and he handed the sketchbook to her to make it easier. "Oh, may I?" She traced her fingers over the lines he had drawn. "What is it that they are playing with?"

The colorful bead didn't reveal itself well in shades of black and white. "It's a bead. Betty broke one of Clarinda's necklaces, and she let me take the pieces. Raccoons like pretty things."

Mary Anne turned the pages slowly, studying each sketch in detail. However, she didn't pause to read his jottings, and he felt strangely aggrieved.

She turned at last to a blank page and sighed. "I want to see more. How many of these books do you have?"

"I'm working on my third volume." At least three days a week, he worked on them. Even in the coldest days of winter, he had gone in hunt of animals that ventured out in the snow.

She paged back to the mother raccoon with her babies, four identical faces peering up at him. "I've never seen a live raccoon before. They look like robbers, don't they, with masks on their faces? And I guess they do rob things, if they grab beads. Daddy always said God must have a sense of humor." The laughter vanished from her face. "Or maybe not." Shutting the book, she handed it back to Wallace. "I was in the cemetery when I saw the cabin." Her shoulders slumping, she stared pensively at the woods.

How could he stay upset with this woman, who took the same joy he did in God's creatures and escaped outside to find peace when she was grieving? He wanted to ask about her father, but she hadn't mentioned him even when he brought up the subject of his own parents' deaths.

Time had passed since then, so he decided to risk it. "Your father must have been a special man."

"He was. There's not a day goes by when I don't think about something he said or did, and I start missing him all over again." When she looked at Wallace, tears glittered in her blue eyes. "Tell me, does it get any easier?"

"Some people will tell you that time heals all wounds. And logic tells you that parents will die before their children do. But you and I, we're too young to have lost both of our parents already. It's not natural."

He heard the rise in his voice, and she began crying openly.

"Aw, shucks, Mary Anne. It is better now than when they first died. Some days I hardly think about them, if at all. Every so often, I think of them so much I almost hurt inside. And other days, like when I see the baby animals, or when Clarinda had her children, I realize that life goes on. That's the way God intends it." In his attempt to offer hope to Mary Anne, he had revealed more of himself than he had to most other people.

"We're born, we live, we die," she said. "That would be sad, except isn't that how Paul describes the gospel? 'Moreover, brethren, I declare unto you the gospel which I preached unto you, which also ye have received, and wherein ye stand…how that Christ died for our sins according to the scriptures. And that he was buried, and that he rose again the third day according to the scriptures.'"

Mary Anne continued quoting from the fifteenth chapter of the first letter to the Corinthians, where Paul mentioned Jesus's appearances after His resurrection. She didn't hesitate as she continued quoting verse after verse, not making a mistake that Wallace could tell.

"'If in this life only we have hope in Christ, we are of all men most miserable.'" She stopped her recitation in mid-chapter. "I've always liked that verse. Without the hope of Jesus's resurrection, and our own eternal life, we're as miserable as everyone else. Thank you for reminding me that death isn't the end of it. Daddy is in Heaven, waiting for me."

Wallace hadn't reminded her of anything; rather, she had taken him back to the hope they shared because of the resurrection. Sunday school teachers had pounded into his head the short passage about Jesus' death, burial and resurrection, and preachers frequently read from the passage before they partook of the Lord's Supper. But Wallace had never heard anyone else quote half the chapter without a pause, not even the pastor. She rose several degrees in his estimation.

Standing, she explored the outside of the cabin, rubbing her hands along the logs, her fingers poking through the chinks that needed attention before winter. He strolled behind her, studying her response to the place generations of his family had called home.

"Was this your family's home during the Revolutionary War?"

"That house tumbled down eventually. The ruins are close to here, though, if you want to see them one day."

Why had he said that, when he came to the cabin seeking solitude? "My great-grandfather built this cabin. My parents lived here until they built their own place. Clarinda was born here."

Mary Anne grunted. She had reached the back wall and stopped at the chimney, feeling the smooth surface of the rock. Year-round, even when a hot fire burned inside, the outside walls stayed fairly cool to the touch. They made their way back to the front. "It's small. As small as our apartment was." Mary Anne spread her arms as if to she could circle the cabin in her embrace.

Wallace laughed. "And yet families with eight children lived in places not much bigger than this."

"But you come out here to be alone." She nodded her head as if to emphasize the point.

Had he made her feel unwelcome? "Well…" Heat rose in his cheeks, and he started to turn away, then worried that movement would reinforce his unsociable attitude.

"Your secret's safe with me," she whispered. "If I could have escaped to a quiet place, away from my loud neighbors, I would have gone in a minute." She shuffled her feet. "In fact, I enjoyed having the house to myself this morning, although your family has been wonderful." She opened the oval watch hanging from a chain around her neck. "It's later than I thought. I better head back to the house before Clarinda gets home and wonders where I disappeared to."

A will-o'-the-wisp, no more substantial than a feather carried by the wind, Mary Anne buttoned her coat and headed down the path. She turned around once to wave.

Her departure left a void Wallace didn't care to examine too closely.

Chapter 8

Mary Anne sat wedged between Winnie and Wallace on the Tuttle family pew. A small plaque on the end of the pew even carried their names. Clarinda had seen her running her fingers over the brass, and she read it aloud: "'In loving memory of Mr. and Mrs. George Tuttle, 1919.'" How many generations of Tuttles had sat in this same pew? Probably they had worshipped the Lord in this sanctuary since the first Sunday it opened.

As a girl, Mary Anne had found it difficult to stay still. She learned better when her hands were busy doing something else. Daddy had allowed her to sit on the floor, coloring to her heart's content. At home, she memorized chunks of scripture by listening to Daddy read from their Bible while she played with her dolls. That Bible had taken its place in her suitcase, although she didn't expect to use it.

Howie, Arthur and Betty stood with the other children in the back, awaiting the Palm Sunday procession. The organist stopped playing, and a hush descended over the congregation. In the back, feet shuffled and whispering voices conveyed last-minute instructions to the children.

"This is Betty's first time." Wallace leaned over and spoke into Mary Anne's ear.

"I know," she whispered back. "She hasn't stopped talking about it all week."

Howard looked at them, and they both sat back, quiet, like two children caught doing something naughty.

The organist played an introduction, and warbling high voices sang off-key as the smallest children marched down the center aisle, holding the hands of the older children. Howie held Betty's hand, and they each waved a bunch of marsh grass that grew by rivers. Somewhere they might have palm branches for Easter, but not here in northern Vermont. When Betty reached the row containing her family, she dropped Howie's hand and waved.

The children sang, the words coming clearer as they neared the front. "First let me hear how the children stood round his knee, and I shall fancy his blessing resting on me…"

"Tell me the stories of Jesus." Nodding, hungry for the stories of Jesus that she had loved since childhood, Mary Anne swallowed against the lump that had formed in her throat. Oh, to have the innocence of these little ones as they climbed on His knees.

The children remained at the front of the sanctuary while the hymn singing continued. "All Glory, Laud and Honor" followed "Hosanna, Loud Hosanna." As the songs of praise lifted to the heavens, Mary Anne rejoiced in her decision to come to church to worship on this day. A careful application of makeup hid the bruises which had nearly faded. A few ladies of the church also used a bit of lipstick, a brush of color on their cheeks.

Clarinda had provided Mary Anne with a crocheted hat

that clung to her head. A thin black band around the rim and a larger band at the crown set off the pure white thread, a stylish design appropriate for this setting. It also hid most of her hair. A stranger in a small town, she didn't expect to escape notice. But neither did she want to leave a bad impression. From what she had learned about the Tuttles, branches of the family spread across the northeast. Maybe the congregation would think she was a distant relative come for a visit.

Whatever the danger of discovery, Mary Anne had to attend church on Palm Sunday and Easter. Even if her behavior during the past few months had led her into waters few Christians ever navigated, she felt compelled to worship her risen Savior, to celebrate all He had done for her. For her, Mary Anne Laurents or Marabelle Lamont, whatever she called herself. *And Lord, next year, let me worship You in the place where You want me to begin my life over again.*

Mary Anne looked down the pew, at Betty fidgeting in her mother's lap, at Arthur and Howie trading crayons across the floor, a scuffle halted by a stern look from their father. Wallace shook his head and returned his attention to the preacher. His pen drummed a light rhythm on his Bible, as if itching to sketch the people at worship, etching the pastor's words into his memory.

The pastor announced the passage for his sermon, the twenty-first chapter of Matthew. He called for the congregation to rise in honor of the reading of God's Word.

Wallace held out his Bible to share with her, and she slipped her hand beneath the left half of the Bible, but didn't look down. Instead, she mouthed the words with the preacher. *And if any man say ought unto you, ye shall say, The Lord hath need of them; and straightway he will send them.*

The Lord *needed* them? The Lord who created the universe needed that particular donkey and colt? She couldn't imagine that God needed something she had.

And what did I do with all the money God gave to Daddy and me? I ran away with it.

The pastor finished reading, and dresses rustled as the congregation settled in their seats.

A slight scratching noise grabbed her attention. Wallace had unfolded a sheet of paper on top of his Bible, probably to take quick sermon notes.

The paper fell to the floor and both of them reached for it. Mary Anne caught it, glancing at it as she handed it back. He wasn't taking sermon notes, or notes of any kind. Instead he was drawing again. Birds, the cat, the children as they marched down the aisle, a dozen miniatures danced across the page.

She handed it to him without reaction, but he still blushed. Of course he knew she had seen.

Not wanting to embarrass either one of them any further, Mary Anne redirected her attention to the preacher. Only strict discipline kept her from gazing at Wallace. Arthur handed her a picture he had drawn. His donkey and the man riding it consisted of stick figures, but the other people in the drawing were still recognizable. The Jerusalem crowd consisted of three children of varying sizes, two men and two women, one of them with a white hat. She pointed to the picture and then at herself.

Delighted, Arthur grinned. "For you." He whispered in the lowest possible voice, but his father glared at him and he buried his face in an empty sheet of paper.

Today, with children at her feet and all around her, Mary Anne experienced Jesus's ride into Jerusalem in a new way. She could imagine how hard those parents tried to keep their children from bothering the man they believed would free Israel from Rome's yoke. The children didn't listen, but ran forward, hundreds of them, surrounding Jesus on all sides. How happy they made Jesus. So much so that when those spoil-sports, the Pharisees, said Jesus should scold the children, He said that if He did, the very rocks would cry out.

This Palm Sunday was that kind of day as well. Vermont's mountains rang with praise to the Lord. Today made Mary Anne look forward, someday, to children of her own, maybe a girl in pigtails and a boy with wavy brown hair and gray eyes like Wallace's.

Those children would look perfect sitting in a church pew like this one, polished maple covered with soft velvet seats, and a man sketching pictures at her side.

Wallace couldn't believe he had allowed Mary Anne to glimpse his silly pictures. His father had rapped his fingers whenever he caught Wallace in the act of drawing instead of listening to the pastor's rambling sermons. Their current preacher's dynamic style should have cured Wallace of his childish habit, but he still listened better while his hands moved.

He hadn't given in to that temptation for a long time, however. The woman next to him was to blame. If he drew pictures, he could keep his mind *on* the sermon and off Mary Anne. After he folded the paper and flattened it with the base of his pencil, he closed his Bible, picture and all. His watch told him that the sermon should be drawing to a close. Tasty aromas from the church basement testified to the ham dinner to follow. Secretly he wished a quick end to the service, so that he could escape the growlings of his stomach, his inattention and Mary Anne's presence.

The sermon dragged on for five more minutes. The pastor appealed to the congregation to rededicate themselves to serving the Lord with all their hearts, but kept the invitation hymn to two verses of "A Charge to Keep I Have." Maybe the man was human after all, ready for a meal.

Wallace noticed the curious looks directed at Mary Anne,

as well as her discomfort with the scrutiny. Putting Betty down so that she could run after her brothers, Clarinda stepped into the gap. "Yes, this is a family friend. Mary Anne Laurents…" She had given them the opportunity they needed to get away quietly.

Wallace wished he could whisk Mary Anne to the front of the line to avoid casual chitchat, but that privilege was reserved for the older members of the congregation. Families with small children went next. Howard corralled the boys while Clarinda went ahead with Betty, deflecting questions about their mystery guest.

Without speaking his intent, Wallace delayed leaving the sanctuary until it had largely emptied. They came at the end of the line greeting the pastor.

He shook Wallace's hand while he smiled at Mary Anne. "How lovely to have you visiting with us today, Miss…?"

"Laurents. Mary Anne Laurents."

The pastor turned his attention to Wallace, as if seeking additional information. What to say? Even though the other members of the congregation had already left the room, he lowered his voice. "I'm afraid I ran into Miss Laurents's car earlier this month. Taking her in was the least we could do, but she's a trifle shy." Where the desire to protect her from curiosity came from, Wallace didn't know, but it was there. "Anything you can do to silence the gossip mill will be appreciated."

Mary Anne's smile held the dawn's brilliance in it. Even her hair looked beautiful beneath the tasteful cap Clarinda had fashioned for her. In her no-nonsense way, she had handed it to their guest. "I thought you might like to have a new hat for Easter." Mary Anne had taken hold of it like grass soaking up rain after a drought.

An hour later, after they finished their meal, Wallace wondered why he had worried so about Mary Anne. She talked easily with his nephews. When people stopped by to meet her, she showed them Arthur's picture. Since the picture included her as a member of the family, people took it at face value. To those few who ventured further questions, she said, "I'm visiting from out of state." She didn't mention New York, Wallace noticed, although people aware of regional accents would pick up on her Brooklyn roots easily enough.

Someone mentioned Boston, and the speculation spread from one person to another. He caught her smiling as she heard the rumor start. She nodded, as if pleased. Some day he hoped she would trust him enough to tell him about her past.

Worshipping the Lord with her sufficed for today. And she truly had worshipped, singing and quoting scripture and listening to the pastor's sermon when she hadn't been peeking at his drawings. At the beginning of Passion Week, he rejoiced that she had chosen to join them at church.

Even after tramping through the woods yesterday to the point of exhaustion, Wallace couldn't keep Mary Anne out of his mind. Her attendance at church pleased him more than he cared to admit.

After the meal ended, the family took the road from town and over the bridge. Mary Anne shuddered as they passed the point where the accident had occurred. On impulse, he asked, "Do you want to come to the cabin for the rest of the afternoon? We could grab some sandwiches and go to the river to watch the animals."

He didn't miss the gleam in Clarinda's eyes, or the pleased smirk on Winnie's face. Even Howard shook his head. Wallace wished he had chosen a less public forum for inviting Mary Anne to join him.

She blinked and looked down at her clothes. *Stupid, Wallace.* The lady had dressed for church, and he was asking her to wade along the muddy banks of the river?

"I have overshoes in the back." Clarinda addressed his

concern. "You won't want to ruin those lovely shoes." She looked over Mary Anne's head at Wallace. "And I'm sure my brother has an extra sweater or coat at the cabin in case you get cold."

"And dresses will wash." Mary Anne smiled. "Very well. That sounds like fun."

A few feet later, Howard brought the car to a halt at the footpath leading to the cabin.

"Don't worry. I'll bring her safely home before dark."

Wallace added a silent promise, one made only to himself. He'd keep her safe, wherever and whatever that involved.

Chapter 9

Wallace wasn't sure who was having the most fun today, him or Mary Anne. The two women had spent Friday preparing the Easter eggs for the hunt, and Mary Anne appeared as excited as any of the children. The new skirt Clarinda had sewn for her hung to a modest calf-length and protected her skin from the brambles they encountered in the fields.

They crossed the designated field in parallel lines, hiding the prepared eggs in promising spots.

"You do know we'll be eating egg salad and deviled eggs for the next week, don't you?" Wallace asked.

Mary Anne's laughter was as bright as the red egg he held in his hand. "And the egg whites may be red or green or blue. It's fun. And to have a place like this to hide eggs…" She parted the dry stalks of last year's grass and tucked an egg in the empty space. "This is wonderful."

"I can see that one from over here." Not only was the egg bright yellow, Mary Anne had laid it on top of the grasses.

"That's so the littlest ones can find it all by themselves. In fact, I was wondering…What do you think about making part of the field just for the children who are under four?"

"They hunt in pairs."

She looked disappointed that he had dismissed her suggestion so easily. "We tried it that way a few times, but they wander away. The parents insist on the pairs. But I like your idea of hiding a few where the little ones can find them without help." He gestured with his next egg, a light purple color, and nestled it in the dirt behind him.

Wallace and Mary Anne were superintending the Easter egg hunt while the mothers put together a meal for all the families involved. The children arrived ahead of time. "Where did all these children come from?" she asked.

"They live west of the river. At times people have voted about making this side of the river a separate town, West Maple Notch. But we have ties to town too close to want to change it."

Children clustered around them, eager for the baskets. Decorations consisted of soft grass at the bottom and colorful bows Mary Anne had added.

Mary Anne's merry blue eyes darted in his direction, her body swirling in a dance-like move as she lined the children in pairs, older with the younger. "Now, be sure you share your eggs with the little ones."

Howie rolled his eyes but took Betty's hand. The children—Reids and Tuttles as well as the three Finches among them—formed a ragged line. Starting at opposite ends of the line, Wallace and Mary Anne passed out baskets.

Wallace kept the children in check. "There are some rules to the hunt. All the eggs are hidden in this field, so if we see any of you going over the fence, you won't find any eggs, and you're also out of the hunt. Stay with your partner. All eggs found by either one of you counts in your total, and you'll each get a prize."

Mary Ann held high a red egg. "Who knows what day tomorrow is?"

"Easter!" A dozen voices called.

"And what are we celebrating on Easter?" Mary Anne continued with her questions as if she was teaching a class. Had she been a Sunday school teacher?

Again voices rose in response. "Jesus rose from the dead!"

"And why did Jesus die?" She turned around slowly, so that every child could see the red egg.

One of the younger children, not even old enough for kindergarten, piped up. "'Cause He had to die for our sins. Don't you know that, Miss Laurents?"

"Of course I do. My daddy used to say—"

Wallace was sure he was the only one who noticed the tears behind the words.

"—that we dye eggs red at Easter time to remind us that Jesus shed His blood on the cross." She tapped the outside of the egg. "Do you hear anything?"

Faces around her scrunched in concentration. They had been too busy talking to hear the light tap.

"Listen again." This time the group was quiet enough to hear her nails hitting the hard shell. "The shell on the egg is hard, like the big rock that was rolled in front of the grave where Jesus lay. And nobody, not the priests, not the Roman soldiers, thought He could ever get out. But then, on Sunday morning…"

With her hardest tap yet, at the top of the egg, the shell cracked, and she peeled it off in two easy strips. "God raised Jesus out of the grave! He rolled that stone away as easily as I peeled this egg."

She was a natural-born storyteller, the children her entranced audience.

"So when you eat your eggs this week, think about how God cracked the grave open so Jesus could come out."

Wallace was impressed. He had learned about Easter traditions at school, but he hadn't heard many people connect the decorated eggs with the gospel story so simply or so easily. Sparkling with joy as she was today, she was so pretty he could hardly stand it.

"Are you ready?" she asked.

The line of children tensed for the start of the hunt.

"Go!" Wallace used his thunderous voice and the children scattered across the field.

Mary Anne clapped her hands with joy at the sight. Wallace laughed with her. He wouldn't mind a lifetime of that kind of laughter.

Mary Anne couldn't believe she had been in Maple Notch only a month and a day. After taking part in the Easter egg hunt a week ago, she had decided this community held nothing for her to fear. Only her bleached and bobbed hair stood out as different from the residents, and time would take care of that.

Today promised to be a good day. Wallace had invited her to go with him in search of more wildlife this morning. They left the house at dawn, unlike their previous two trips. Her loud noises, magnified in the stillness of the morning air, had scared away half of the usual visitors to the pond. He had apologized multiple times for the paucity of wildlife. Except for her disappointment in missing the raccoons at play, she hadn't cared. Watching the silvery fish wiggle through the water brought her a great deal of joy. Oh, to have Wallace's skill with a paper and pencil.

Silence didn't matter as much when they went in search of animals and birds at other times of the day. When he found signs of an animal's passage, he put a finger to his lips and froze. Even his breathing slowed down at those times, and she imitated him. What would they see today?

He fixed breakfast when they returned to the cabin. His offering of biscuits and gravy brought laughter to her lips.

"I had to try it. I think it tastes okay, but I hope you like it." He looked on anxiously while she dug her fork into the biscuit.

Mary Anne steeled herself to hide her disgust if she found it distasteful. But as in so many other things about this man, he proved her wrong. "Mmm, that's good."

"You don't have to sound so surprised." A smile lit his face. "And here is the bacon to go with it. No eggs, you'll see."

She laughed at that. "Good. At this point of the year I always feel like I'll be happy never to see an egg except baked in a cake. Give me a few weeks, and I'll be happy to eat some of your special fried eggs again."

They ate together in peace and headed out again. "I thought I spotted a bald eagle the other day. It was at a distance, so I brought my binoculars today," Wallace said.

"Our national bird? The one we see on the top of flag poles and stuff like that? White head, with a brown body?" Mary Anne had only seen one live eagle in her lifetime, when Daddy had taken her to the Bronx Zoo. The feathers on that eagle's head were the color of goldenrod.

"That's the one."

"And you're saying the bald eagle is—" What was the word Wallace used to describe it? "—endangered?"

"It is. That's why it's so important that I report the sighting to the Audubon Society, if I confirm it today."

Imagine the idea of saying a bird could be in danger of disappearing from the planet. Wallace said they were dying out, fewer and fewer of nesting pairs. The day might come when there wouldn't be any bald eagles anywhere in the entire country.

The difficulties Mary Anne faced paled by comparison to extinction. To think she dreamed of flying away to safety like a bird. That didn't always solve problems. "What are some of the other birds that are endangered?"

Wallace cocked his head at her. "So you're interested in our birds? There's the spruce grouse, the grasshopper sparrow…"

He lost her after about the third name. Some of the birds sounded vaguely familiar, especially the sparrow. How could the birds that littered the ground in Central Park and even here in Vermont be in danger?

Wallace wasn't done with his list. "…Henslow sparrow…"

"Hen's what?"

"The Henslow sparrow."

"But you already said the sparrow was endangered. I have a hard time believing that. I see them everywhere."

"There are several kinds of sparrows, but the two species that are dying out are the Grasshopper and the Henslow."

"Grasshopper?" What a strange name.

"His song sounds like an insect. I guess that's why they named it that. They're hard to distinguish from other sparrows. They're brown, with an unmarked, buff-colored breast. The male's head is darker, with a pale middle stripe. The problem is, the Henslow looks a lot like it."

Mary Anne didn't know how to tell them all apart.

"Here, let me show you." Even though he only had a pencil, no colors, his drawing suggested the differences between the birds. The pictures he drew were larger than life, the two species side by side in his sketchbook.

Holding the sketchbook close to her face, she memorized the details. "How can you tell the difference between them if you're far away? I see a bird like either one of these and think 'sparrow,' and that's the end of it."

He shrugged. "Being close does help. Binoculars, too. The

more you study them, the easier it is to tell the difference. For instance—" He paused, holding a finger to his lips. "Listen." The word came out on the merest whisper of sound.

Crickets thrummed the air. A slow wind stirred a few leaves on the trees. "I hear leaves in the wind, and grass rustling, a dog barking in the distance, crickets."

Wallace lifted a finger. "Ah, but you see. Those aren't crickets. They're not even grasshoppers. It's the grasshopper sparrow." He held the binoculars to his face and scanned the horizon. "I see them now, over there close to that fence post." He pointed before handing Mary Anne the binoculars.

After fiddling with the glasses to adjust the lenses, she zeroed in on the pair of birds. "I see the head and the light breast. I even see the stripe on their breasts." Her excitement increased. Turning the glasses further afield, she nearly shouted. "And then there's a Henslow! At least I think that's what it is."

"Where?"

She handed him the binoculars. "A little bit to the left. Farther away from the field."

He turned his head, fiddled with the magnification, while a smile formed around his mouth. "Why, Mary Anne, you're right. You're a natural-born birder. You should join the Audubon Society and come to the next meeting."

The Audubon Society? The audacity—and possibilities—of such a suggestion thrilled Mary Anne down to her toes.

Wallace didn't repeat his suggestion that Mary Anne come to the Audubon Society with him. Even if she were interested, she might leave before the next meeting.

The plan for today was a better idea. In addition to the private skating lessons Preston Nash offered at the converted grist mill, he opened the rink to the public several times a week. All day Saturday was one of those times.

Today the church was sponsoring the annual ice skating party, scheduled in mid-spring as usual. Winnie had invited Mary Anne to go skating with her, and she had agreed. They both had tiny feet, and Mary Anne could fit into an old pair of Winnie's skates. The two of them left for the ice rink earlier than the rest of the family.

"I don't know what we'll do with that girl." Clarinda shook her head, expressing her concern for their sister. "She always says she's done her homework, but it hasn't been all that long since I was at the seminary. I always had plenty to do, without spending hours and hours every day on the ice."

Clarinda and Wallace both dedicated themselves to study, a passion they inherited from their grandmother. "Face it, sis. Both of us liked school. Winnie is satisfied with getting by. Her heart's on the ice."

"What Grandmother Clara would have to say about that, I don't know." Clara Farley Tuttle had founded the Maple Notch Female Seminary more than sixty years ago.

"She'd probably be glad that Winnie can go out and skate and compete. She wanted women to have the same opportunities as men, after all. Remember the first time she voted?"

Watching Grandmother Tuttle cast the first ballot in the 1920 election—she voted for Warren Harding, of course— had helped Wallace understand women's suffrage in a way lectures never managed to do.

Clarinda nodded, but her mind had wandered from the subject. "I'm surprised you let Mary Anne slip out of here without you tagging along."

Howie raced in, in time to hear his mother's remark. "Wallace and Mary Anne sitting in a tree…" He said the familiar words in a high, singsong voice.

"Howard Aaron Finch, Jr., stop that right now." Clarinda's warning came too late.

Wallace turned as hot as a sauna while the rest of the family laughed.

Chapter 10

Wallace recovered his voice. "The social will start without us if we don't get going." Without waiting for any further comments from the peanut gallery, he slung his skates over his shoulder and opened the door.

"Not so fast." Clarinda shoved a pan of brownies into his hands. "Take these to the truck. Sure you don't want to drive with us?"

Wallace shook his head. After Howie's remarks, he'd welcome the solitude. "I'll take the cross country route. It's more direct. I'll get there before you if I hustle."

His sketchbook perched on the windowsill beside the coat rack. His hand hovered over it, the magnet of habit drawing him toward it.

Clarinda saw the direction of his glance. "Don't. You'll find some Winslow sparrow—"

"Henslow," Wallace corrected.

"—and stop to take a look and before you know, it will be suppertime."

Wallace almost placed it back on the sill, but he took it anyway. He might find something even more interesting to sketch at the ice rink. Some*one,* with blond hair turning brown and a swirling blue skating skirt.

Mary Anne hoped to learn some basic techniques before the others arrived. Ice skating couldn't be that much different from the roller skating she had enjoyed as a girl. The thin blade beneath the boot she was lacing made her doubt it. Maybe she shouldn't venture on the ice today, after finally healing from the accident. What if she hurt herself all over again? Her fingers paused, ready to undo the laces.

Winnie had already fled to the ice to warm up. Mary Anne didn't know where she belonged, on the ice or among the women bringing food for the party. She was helpless on skates and in the kitchen. To hear Winnie tell it, people in Maple Notch were practically born with ice skates on their feet.

Overhead, the light in the office went out. In the quiet of the darkness feet plodded on a rickety wooden staircase before a salt-and-pepper-haired man came to the bench where Mary Anne sat, her skates half-tied.

"You haven't moved since you came in with Winnie." He took a spot next to Mary Anne.

"You must be Preston Nash." Winnie talked about her skating mentor all the time. "I'm Mary Anne Laurents. I've been staying at the Tuttle farm."

He simply smiled, leaving Mary Anne to wonder how much Winnie had told him about their unexpected guest. "I'm sure Winnie meant well when she invited you today, but as you can see, she forgets everything else when she's on the ice."

"I've been watching her. She's amazing."

They sat in companionable silence, watching Winnie glide across the ice for a couple of minutes, her skates skimming the surface easily. A spurt across the ice led to a jump that took her so high in the air that a toddler could have walked beneath her without being touched.

"She'll do." Preston nodded his head a single time.

A universe of approval lay beneath those two words.

"But I expect you want to learn more about skating before the church descends on us." He nodded at her partly laced skates.

No wonder Winnie valued this man. He understood things left unspoken. Bending over, Mary Anne finished lacing her right boot.

Before she could start on the left foot, Mr. Nash stopped her. "Let me help you." He tugged the laces on the boot she had finished, tightening them so that her leg felt snug. He looped the extra length of the shoelace around her leg once before knotting it in front. "You need 'er tight and snug like that, you see, to support your ankle."

Following his example, she worked on her left foot, and when she finished, he didn't stoop to tighten it any more. "Ready to go?"

He had slipped his skates on while she struggled with the left boot. Although he held her hands as she stood, her ankles wobbled over the thin blades. He walked backward, a feat Mary Anne couldn't imagine doing on skates. She took a tentative step, then another. "It will get easier once you're on the ice."

Mary Anne doubted that. On the ice, what would prevent her feet from sliding out from underneath her while she tumbled down?

The door opened, and Wallace sprinted around the perimeter of the ice until he reached them. Preston nodded in greeting. "I was about to show Miss Laurents the basics of skating, but I will turn that privilege over to you." With a flash in his eyes that was as good as a wink, he placed Mary Anne's hand on the rail that surrounded the rink and waited with her until Wallace changed into his skates. Mr. Nash let go of her hand after Wallace stood, and then he joined Winnie in the center of the ice.

"Do you object to me taking over for Preston?" Wallace stepped onto the ice with ease. "He's the professional among us."

Mary Anne shook her head.

Skating backward, Wallace held out his hands to Mary Anne. His hands tugged her forward, and she lifted her right foot to step onto the ice. A moment later, her left foot joined it, and, to her surprise, she didn't fall.

Laughing, Wallace skated back a few inches. How he managed without lifting his feet, she didn't know. When she lifted her right foot, her left leg buckled and she lurched forward.

"Steady!" Wallace held her hands tight to keep her from falling. "Skating's not like walking. You push forward with one leg, then the other. Like this." He switched sides, so that he stood next to her, slipping one arm behind her to hold her hand on her far side. "Do like I do."

She gave her left leg a hesitant push and she glided forward.

"That's it. Keep going."

Left, right, left…the rhythm reminded her of roller skating. "I'm doing it!"

"You're a natural." Wallace dropped her right hand, then her left, and she glided as far as forward momentum could carry her. She tottered for a moment before Wallace gently took hold of her hands, facing her again as he skated backward. "Let's try that again." He kept his hands on hers, only the lightest of touches, and she began again. "We like to skate to the song 'Faith is the Victory.' Do you know it?"

The tempo of the song made it easier to move her legs in rhythm. Wallace whirled to her side again, taking only her right hand with his left, while they completed the circle of the rink. As they approached the entrance, Wallace let go. The gate rushed at her. "How do I stop?"

"Like this." Wallace made a gradual turn, scraping one skate across the ice.

As Wallace demonstrated the stop, Howie rushed onto the ice and crashed into both of them.

One moment, Wallace was gliding across the ice, watching Mary Anne skate on her own as if she were born on skates. The next, Howie jumped onto the ice in front of Mary Anne, knocking her down first, before crashing into Wallace. The three of them landed on their behinds.

Howie jumped up first. "Good to see you skating, Miss Mary Anne!" He raced across the ice. Winnie escaped a similar fate by sidestepping him.

Shaking his head, Wallace got to his feet. He hadn't let Howie catch him that way for years. Mary Anne remained sprawled on the ice, first lifting one shaky arm, then the other.

"Are you all right?" He helped her to her feet. Although she appeared not to be seriously injured, she was shaken from the fall. Wallace helped her to the edge of the ice and pulled a pair of blade protectors from his pocket. "Let me put these on your skates. They'll make it easier to walk and keep the blades from getting dull."

Bending over, he lifted one foot that dangled only inches from the floor. He snapped the protector in place, then added the second guard. Mary Anne trembled so that he worried she would fall down before he finished. "I'm so sorry." His voice dropped. "You must still be sore from the accident."

When she leaned against his side, a desire to protect this woman from all harm swelled up in his heart. On the bench, he basked in the warmth of her closeness. Preston appeared without speaking, offering her a cup of hot cocoa.

"Thank you." By the time she emptied the cup, color had returned to her cheeks, and about a dozen people were on the ice.

"Are you all right? Do you want to see the doctor?" Wallace jerked his head in the direction of the door, where Dr. Landrum was entering with his family.

"No, I'm fine, but I'll leave the ice for those who are more experienced with it."

Wallace's concern about lingering soreness from the accident brought him to his feet, but at her decision, he sat again.

At that, Mary Anne shook her head. "Don't stay here on my account. You deserve a break from all your work. And you might not get another chance to skate until next winter. Go out there and have fun."

Wallace prepared to refuse when a familiar voice almost shouted in his ear.

"Wallace Tuttle, as I live and breathe. I haven't seen you since graduation."

Wallace would know that voice anywhere—Margaret Landrum, the doctor's daughter. Mary Anne shrank back as Margaret's shadow fell on her.

"And you must be Dad's mystery patient at the Tuttle farm." Margaret remained oblivious to her reaction. "I'm Margaret Landrum." She stuck her hand out for a shake, and Mary Anne had no choice but to oblige.

"Mary Anne Laurents." Mary Anne inched away from Wallace's side. "Go ahead. I'm sure you have much to discuss." She practically pushed him to his feet and into Margaret's arms.

Pasting a smile on his face, Wallace escorted an all-too-willing Margaret onto the ice.

Chapter 11

Wallace stepped onto the ice with Margaret. Since their high school graduation almost five years ago, he hadn't seen her for more than a few minutes at holiday church services. When she was a student and boarder at the Maple Notch Female Seminary, Margaret had spent a lot of time with the Tuttle family. Like many other promising students, she had gone out of state for further education.

"And how is medical school going?" he asked.

"Well." She was doing better than well. She was attending Geneva College, the same school where Elizabeth Blackwell, the first female physician in the United States, had trained. Even as a teen, Margaret had known she would follow in her father's footsteps. Grandma Clara would have been so pleased. The few opportunities for girls with Margaret's kind of talent had convinced his grandmother of the need to start the seminary all those years ago.

Margaret had changed in other ways as well. She wore

trousers—a rarity for women in Maple Notch—and she had bobbed her hair. "You look…different." His hand reached for his head even as he told himself not to emphasize it.

She reached up to touch her hair. While it was short, it was still her own light brown color. "I've been wearing it this way for several years. It's much easier."

They made their way around the rink twice. Margaret didn't feel nearly as light in his arms as Mary Anne had. He glanced to the side of the rink, where he could see she had exchanged her skates for her shoes. Gone was his opportunity to coax her onto the ice one more time.

"I fear I have gotten out of shape." Margaret bent over, wheezing. "I need to spend more time on the ice while I'm here this summer. Will I be seeing you?"

She was being as forward as any girl Wallace had met at university. He shook his head. "I doubt I'll have the time. I am a hardworking man."

"You always were serious." Her smile took the sting out of the words.

They sat on the bench abandoned by Mary Anne only minutes ago. As Margaret reached to untie her left skate, she scooted closer to him. In a lowered voice, she asked, "So are you serious about Miss Laurents?"

"Mary Anne?" Long experience with Margaret kept Wallace from feeling affronted by her question.

"Is there another Miss Laurents about?" A light laugh accompanied the question.

"It's none of your business, you know." Why Wallace didn't assert a negative escaped him, except Margaret might take that as an open door for her to waltz through.

Two legs peeking beneath a slim blue skirt came to a stop in front of the spot where Wallace sat. Dainty brown oxfords encased tiny feet. Only one woman besides Winnie had feet that small.

"Would either of you like hot cocoa?" Mary Anne waited in front of them like a restaurant waitress, carrying a tray that held several steaming mugs. Wallace looked up into her face, her cloudless blue eyes, a slight smile lifting the edge of her lips.

"Yes, thank you." He gulped the first swallow so fast it burned his throat.

"No, thanks." Margaret put her skates away and stood. "I see some old friends I want to catch up with." She bounded away.

Mary Anne hesitated before continuing around the railing.

"I was afraid you might leave." Wallace searched for something to convince her to put the tray down and join him on the bench. "Why don't you sit down and rest that leg? I hope you can come out to the cabin next week. I've spotted some new birds you might like to see."

The smile lurking around the edges of her mouth burst into a grin. "I would enjoy that very much. But for now—" she lifted an elbow to emphasize the tray in her hands "—I'd better hand out the hot cocoa before it cools into chocolate milk."

Wallace watched her straight back, the graceful movement of her skirt swishing around her legs, the simple bun resting at the top of her blouse's sailor collar. The natural color of her hair peeked out at the roots, a shade of brown somewhere between an acorn and a walnut. She changed day by day, and Wallace liked what he saw.

"I don't know if I want to wear these." Mary Anne twirled, studying the fit of the blue jeans Clarinda had lent her. "They cover my legs nicely, but I just don't feel right wearing them. This—" she patted her favorite blue jersey skirt waiting on the hanger "—has done a yeoman's duty since you adjusted it to fit me."

"If I know my brother, Wallace will be dragging you over

mountains and rivers in search of those birds. Your legs will be scratched, if not worse."

Poison oak, poison ivy, poison sumac. Wallace had pointed out each plant and warned her against them. He was almost surprised she didn't already recognize them, but she hadn't encountered them on her few trips to Central Park with Daddy.

A crazy thought crossed Mary Anne's mind. Pulling the waistband of the blue jeans up as high as she could, she tugged the skirt over her head and past her waist.

From her spot on the bed, Clarinda laughed. "I've done that with Betty a time or two, in the winter, when it was too cold to go outside with only a skirt. It's probably still chilly up in the mountains."

The skirt barely fit over the blue jeans. The ease of movement she associated with the skirt disappeared beneath the tight constriction of the trousers. The resulting surface resembled a rocky seashore, not at all attractive, and not very practical either.

"The blue jeans it will be, then." Mary Anne took off the skirt, easing it over the places where it caught on the blue jeans before replacing it on the hanger. The sweater was the color of a blue lobelia that went well with the blue jeans, so she didn't change it. Daddy had once said it reminded him of the color of Mary Anne's eyes. Would Wallace notice the same thing? A tiny flame built in her heart at the thought.

"You look like you were born for the woods." Clarinda nodded in approval. "If I hadn't seen the transformation myself, I would never guess you were the same young lady who arrived here last month." Her brown eyes brimmed with warmth.

Mary Anne planned to ride as far as the footpath in the car with the family. Downstairs where the children waited,

Winnie was reading a picture book with animal characters to the boys.

"I think you like that story more than the children do," Clarinda said. "Hurry now, out to the car, before we're late."

Winnie dragged her book bag over her shoulder, her homework done in spite of Clarinda's worries, and raced for the door. "Of course I love it. Milne named the bear for *me,* after all. Winnie-the-Pooh. What is a pooh, I wonder? Some slang word they use in England?"

"You can blame Shakespeare for that word," Clarinda remarked as they climbed into the car.

Mary Anne climbed beside her, grateful for the warmth of the blue jeans.

As the children tumbled into the car, Clarinda said, "Hamlet exclaimed 'Affection! Pooh! You speak like a green girl.' It was one of Wallace's favorite sayings at one time."

Shakespeare and Hamlet. Of course. Only someone with an education like Clarinda's would make the connection between a children's book and Shakespeare. Mary Anne giggled as she made a connection of her own. Her friends had taken her to see a comic opera that she found delightful. "I also heard the word used in a comic opera by Gilbert and Sullivan, *The Mikado.* The Lord High Everything Else was called Pooh-Bah. It sounds kind of like Pooh Bear, doesn't it?" Especially among these Vermonters, who tended to drop *R*s from the ends of words.

"Lord Pooh-Bah?" Arthur laughed.

"Yes, it was a very funny show," Mary Anne said. Soon even little Betty joined in the laughter.

Clarinda stopped the car by the path leading past the cemetery to the cabin, and Mary Anne hopped out. She started humming another melody from *The Mikado.* "'Oh, willow, titwillow, titwillow!'" The song suited a day when she would be searching for birds. Was a titwillow an actual bird, or only one in the imagination of Gilbert and Sullivan? In that case, it was the most endangered species of all. She started laughing.

As had become her habit, Mary Anne paused by the cemetery to think about Daddy for a few minutes. He would enjoy both Winnie-the-Pooh and Pooh-Bah, the Lord High Everything Else. He had a good sense of humor.

Taking the pencil she had started carrying with her, she let her imagination take flight as she drew a titwillow. The bird should have a high crest on his head, she decided, like a crown. His eyes slanted on both sides of the beak. Her mind gave him a white face with a red beak. Quickly she sketched the rest: a fat breast hanging over two spindly legs, wide feet almost like the geese. But she didn't have the skill Wallace did to bring the bird, even an imaginary one, to life.

Flipping back a few pages, she went over the sketches of the endangered birds Wallace had made for her. His sketches made more sense to her than the terse descriptions used in his bird manuals. The Henslow sparrow came to life with his colored pencils in a way that saying it had a "streaked chest, olive nape, and two stripes on the lower face" failed to conjure up. What colors were the stripes? What was a nape? What was considered the lower part of a bird's face? She thought of a bird's head, not its face. But once Wallace showed the details with a few lines with his pencil, she could recognize it through the binoculars immediately.

She reviewed the list as she studied each sketch for details: spruce grouse, upland sandpiper, black tern, common tern, and sedge wren, as well as the sparrows and the eagle she had encountered on their first hike together. He made learning easy.

Mary Anne hoped Wallace would never find out the most important purpose the pictures served.

"Here you are." Wallace had sneaked up on her and startled her. She dropped the sketchbook and it opened to her unfortunate picture of the titwillow.

"What is this?" His broad lips widened in a smile.

"It's a titwillow. You know, 'titwillow, titwillow!' from *The Mikado?*"

"I've heard of it." He grabbed the sketchbook before she could pick it up.

"It's just a bit of foolishness I made up. We were talking about the show this morning, and I wondered what a titwillow might look like."

Wallace leaned his head to one side while he studied it, but she didn't mind. She enjoyed the hours they spent together, whether they were skating on the ice or hiking through the woods looking for Wallace's beloved birds. The longer she stayed in Maple Notch, the less she wanted to leave.

Wallace had hung the picture of the titwillow Mary Anne had sketched on the cabin wall in the spring, back in May. When he moved out, he would add it to his attic room. The childish lines added to its charm, giving it a cartoonlike quality that captured the personality of the Pooh Bah in *The Mikado.* He had seen the comic opera, not the Broadway version which she had enjoyed, but one put on by the University's musical society.

The more time they spent together, the more he enjoyed her company, and the less he could imagine living without her. That day was arriving all too soon.

She had once spoken of leaving by the Fourth of July at the latest. Now the holiday was only three days away. She had more than recovered from the accident; she said she was in the best shape of her life, after all the walking they had done. Her car was repaired, a feat accomplished during a long two days she had spent away from the cabin, repairing the car and making his truck sing.

Nothing kept her here any longer. He took heart from the fact she hadn't mentioned leaving for several weeks.

He could worry about that tomorrow. Today, he found contentment in her presence as they revisited the places where they had seen the most birds. In addition to the time she spent helping Clarinda around the house, Mary Anne had become an integral part of his work. Every specimen he spotted, she verified. Sometimes she even corrected his findings. Because of her help, the book had progressed much faster than he had imagined possible.

He could see the dedication of the book now. "To Mary Anne Laurents, my…" Collaborator. Coworker. Second pair of eyes.

Wife, a voice from deep within said. His traitorous heart jumped at the thought while his brain argued against it. Their close partnership explained his feelings.

A small part of his brain disagreed. *But you've spent time with women all your life. You lived in an all-girls' school when you were in high school. And none of them, not even Margaret Landrum, appealed to you in the same way.*

Those years didn't matter. In high school, he didn't think about girls except to notice the pretty ones.

After college, a man's thoughts turned to family. Mary Anne had certainly dominated his landscape for the past three months. Besides that, she was pretty enough to capture any man's attention.

Someone knocked. "Wallace?"

He shut down the thoughts racing around his mind and opened the door to today's guest.

And perhaps to the future as well.

Chapter 12

Wallace delayed the inevitable parting of his partnership with Mary Anne as long as possible. Her assistance had resulted in his finishing the required research ahead of schedule, in mid-July.

Beside him, she lowered the binoculars and sighed. "No sign of the sedge wren."

She used the name with such familiarity that Wallace chuckled. On their first search to look for the bird, she had no idea what sedge was. Then again, neither had he until he looked up the definition. Sedge referred to ground covering: not grass, but grasslike, with triangular stems and leaves growing in three vertical rows with inconspicuous spikes. He'd sketched both grass and sedge a dozen times before he felt comfortable telling them apart.

Mary Anne studied those same sketches, until she could differentiate between them at a glance. At her suggestion, he planned to include sketches of the birds' habitats in the book.

Disappointment shivered through his veins. "Are you sure?" He reached for the binoculars. When they spotted the nest in May, he'd been so hopeful, and they'd seen the wrens several times since. Slowly he lowered the glasses. "Just the empty nest."

"And feathers. As if they had been torn apart." Mary Anne wiped at her eyes. "How sad. It makes me think about that verse. 'Are not two sparrows sold for a farthing? And one of them shall not fall on the ground without your Father.'"

There she went again, knowing the right Bible verse to quote. She had one of the best memories of anyone he had ever met.

She continued. "Jesus is trying to make us recognize that God cares for us. 'But the very hairs of your head are all numbered. Fear ye not therefore, ye are of more value than many sparrows.' But after watching the birds this summer, it just makes me feel sad." She put a straight line next to the entry for the sedge wren, indicating its absence. "I suppose it makes God feel sad, too."

"At least the bald eagles have fared well this summer." Wallace shrugged his shoulders. "Maybe God doesn't want the United States to lose its national bird."

The glance she threw his way said she didn't appreciate his attempt at humor. "So God plays favorites with birds, then?" She shook her head. "The only bird we haven't checked this week is the sandpiper. Tomorrow." She closed the notebook and tucked it into her satchel.

With unspoken assent, they headed back to the cabin. "I suppose you'll be needing this now." Mary Anne dug the sketchbook out of her pocket. Her fingers brushed his as she placed it in Wallace's hands. Her touch sent a longing through him, a desire to walk hand in hand with her through the trees.

She cocked her head to one side, light playing on skin that

had tanned under the summer sun, a smile offering her lips for exploration.

The sketchbook dropped to the ground as he intertwined his fingers with hers and drew her close. He looked into her eyes, asking permission.

No stop sign appeared, only yield. Beneath the maple trees in the middle of the Vermont woods, he gently touched her lips with his, claiming them as his own.

She stepped back without speaking. She didn't have to. A shy smile lifted her lips, and a new light shone from those lobelia-blue eyes.

On the one time Mary Anne had gone to a speakeasy, she hadn't enjoyed the caresses her drunken escort had planted on her lips. The more alcohol he had imbibed, the more insistent he became. When he refused to take "no" for an answer, she ran out of the basement and found the nearest cab. Later, her friends had laughed at her. "Normal" girls liked a man's kisses.

Wallace's single, gentle kiss had awakened more in her than half a night in the clutches of that gorilla. Not a day had passed through the rest of July and now most of August without her reliving the tender moment.

Oh, how she wished she still had a reason to spend time with Wallace several times a week. How thankful she was that she didn't. If she spent much more time with him, she didn't think she would ever leave Maple Notch.

She had awakened from a dream that ended with that kiss, and it had dominated her thoughts throughout breakfast.

Clarinda cleared her throat, and Mary Anne realized she had been drying the same dish far too long. "Sorry." She placed the plate on top of the stack and slid them into the cabinet.

"You know, you could take the food up to the cabin the

next time Wallace needs some supplies. I have a list, right here." Clarinda waved the page in front of her. "You should get out of the house. Go into town, do some shopping, pick up the things he's asking for. You would understand what he needs more than I do."

"I don't think he wants to see me." Mary Anne's voice sounded as stiff as a boiled shirt, but she didn't know how to change it. "He's been avoiding me."

"And you have stayed in Maple Notch just to help me with my children this summer, and to learn how to can applesauce and corn." Clarinda shook her head. "It hasn't been that long since Howard and I were courting. Things don't change all that much between men and women from one decade to the next." She handed Mary Anne a saucer to dry. "And if it means anything, I'd love to have you for a sister-in-law."

Heat from her embarrassment raced into Mary Anne's cheeks faster than it ever did from the hot steam rising from the dishwater. She held the saucer in front of her face in an effort to hide, although she suspected Clarinda saw everything.

Clarinda handed her the next saucer and pulled the towel down from Mary Anne's face. "Go shopping, and then go see Wallace. He's a man. He's not going to budge, so it's up to you."

Mary Anne's chin rose at that. "I thought the man was supposed to chase the woman." She dried the saucer quickly and added it to the stack in the cabinet.

Clarinda sighed. "Maybe some men. But Wallace has been afraid of his feelings since our parents died. He became the man of the family. Of an entire group of schoolgirls, for that matter. I think it's the only way he survived a difficult time, but it's hurting him now."

"But he's working on his book…" Mary Anne stammered.

"Then he's ready for a break. Believe me."

Mary Anne accepted the shopping list Clarinda handed

to her. *Trapped.* "I'll go tomorrow, then." Before morning, she could come up with an escape plan. She'd been doing it all her life.

After dinner, she joined Clarinda and her husband for the nightly family time. Howard read from the Bible and each child prayed. Even little Betty talked to God, remembering "Kitty's new babies" and "the poor birds that get lost." She had taken Mary Anne's stories about the missing birds to heart, and Wallace was missing it.

They listened to their favorite radio shows on a state-of-the-art Radiola. After the radio hour, Clarinda or Howard read. They read everything. Some books even Betty could understand, adventures about a jungle boy named Mowgli. Howie liked to act out the different animals in the stories. Other stories, by a man named F. Scott Fitzgerald, reminded her of the life she had left behind in New York.

Tonight, she didn't enjoy the family time as much as usual. Even after everyone else retired to bed, Mary Anne remained awake. Instead of finding a way to avoid Clarinda's request, her traitorous heart dreamed of Wallace's reaction when she arrived at his doorstep.

She paced the hallway outside her room, pausing at the foot of the attic stairway. Not for the first time, she wished she dared go into Wallace's room, but he deserved his privacy. She wouldn't intrude unless invited.

In the morning, after Clarinda rebuffed Mary Anne's half-hearted attempt to change her mind, she went to the barn. She ran her hands along the gleaming hood of her coupe. In spite of the many changes Mary Anne had made, she still loved her car. The road option remained open: she could go back to her room, grab her suitcases and take to the road again.

Opening the door, she climbed into the driver's seat. Resting her head against the back of the seat, she imagined the roar of the engine, the glint of sunlight on the paint, the rush of air blowing in her face. She could almost feel the rumble of the road beneath the wheels as trees and towns flashed by. If she made the trip, she would drive during daylight and enjoy the view. Daddy had talked about making a trip one day, driving from Maine to Florida. *Except that would take her past New York.*

Even if New York no longer posed a problem, and while her four and a half months in Vermont seemed like a lifetime to her, her pursuers had long memories and an endless thirst for vengeance. She wasn't sure she wanted to return.

She touched her hair, now with a lot of brown mixed in with the bleached color, with fingernails kept short, practical for work around the house. Her fingers had roughened with the weeks of housework, and her feet hadn't seen high heels for weeks. The Mary Anne who sat in the coupe now was a different woman from the Marabelle who had arrived back in April. She decided to take the family's Model T instead.

A few minutes later, she entered the general store. It carried a variety of art supplies: colored pencils, yes, but also things like chalk, charcoal and watercolors. Mary Anne studied the trays of colored pencils. She knew the colors Wallace needed, the precise shade of the stripe on a Henslow sparrow and the wings of the sedge wren. But she had never imagined that so many choices existed: four shades of brown, more yet of green and blue. After a lengthy perusal, she chose the ones closest to the birds he hoped to recreate on paper.

After she finished shopping, Mary Anne stopped by the soda fountain. "Want an egg cream today, Miss Laurents?"

Mary Anne smiled. During her first visit to the general store, she discovered the soda jerk didn't know the recipe. She told him it was a mixture of chocolate syrup, seltzer water and milk. Neither eggs nor cream were used, which had surprised her the first time she had seen it made.

"Of course." She gave a passing thought to drinking it fast, before the foam went flat, the way purists claimed it should be enjoyed. But today she wanted to savor the flavor slowly.

Maybe her favorite drink would help her build up the courage she needed to face Wallace after he had withdrawn.

Only time would tell if it was a good idea or not.

Chapter 13

Wallace rolled the thin sheets from the outdated Remington No. 2 typewriter that Aunt Flo had given to him. After removing the carbon paper for a second use, he separated the three copies of page two hundred of his manuscript into different stacks. The first copy was destined for the publisher, the second for his own records and the third for extra insurance.

Typing six to eight hours a day in a stifling cabin wasn't Wallace's ideal way to spend a summer. Every day over the past month, and sometimes several times a day, he had longed to return to the cool woods with Mary Anne.

No wonder he struck the typewriter keys hard enough to jam them more than once. When the keys stuck badly, he considered buying a newer machine. Or perhaps Mary Anne's magic hands could fix this one somehow.

Instead he managed to untangle the metal on his own, and he inserted a fresh page onto the roller. Unlike his fellow students, Wallace had used the Remington for most of his college papers. Since he found typing less stressful on his hands than longhand, not to mention easier for his professors to read, it made sense. With years of practice, he had become quite proficient.

But this summer, his typing was worse than it had been on his first term paper. Most pages took two and many three attempts before he had a clean copy. Several times he had to start over when he forgot to mention a sketch.

The sketches had proved troublesome as well. He had contacted the interested editor about colored illustrations, but received a negative response. Color added too much to the cost of printing. Wallace redrew his best sketches in pencil, wishing he had Mary Anne's keen eye to point out any errors.

Of course, Margaret Landrum had offered to help, more than once. She had even sought him out at the cabin, complaining that he should have telephone service if he insisted on living by himself. Resisting the impulse to point out the purpose of solitude, he deterred her suggestion with a comment about smoke signals.

Her smoky gray eyes studied him without blinking. "I get the message. I thought maybe we could find something this summer, but... I left it too late."

After his fumbling apology, she kissed him lightly on the cheek. "Don't worry. Maybe God has an accidental meeting waiting in store for me some day." She lifted her fingers in farewell and disappeared down the path.

Mary Anne filled his thoughts even though he didn't see her. When he realized she visited the cemetery on a regular basis, he dragged a large rock over near the fence for her to sit on. Once in a while, as he headed down the trail, he heard her singing and turned back. She knew where to find him, if she wanted to.

With thoughts of Mary Anne intruding on his work, Wallace would never finish the manuscript before fall, when he had promised to pitch in with the harvest. He needed to keep his mind focused on important things.

The man whose mind is stayed on Thee…The verse popped into Wallace's mind. Mary Anne could quote it word for word.

Resolutely, he stacked together typing paper, carbon, typing paper, carbon and a final sheet of typing paper before inserting it in the typewriter. The pages came out crooked on the far side of the roller. He yanked them from the platen, and a corner of carbon paper tore. After checking it, Wallace decided it wasn't larger than the margins, and shuffled them to make them even.

He inserted them again—success! Someone rapped on the door.

Mary Anne—a new, improved Mary Anne—waited on his doorstep.

The door opened, and Wallace peeked out. Bleary-eyed, with dark circles under his eyes, stubble growing into a thin beard on his chin…all Mary Anne's nervousness about seeing him again disappeared upon first sight.

Without waiting for his invitation, she bustled into the cabin. The single neat spot, three stacks of paper on the low-lying bookshelf, only emphasized the chaos he had made of the cabin. Dishes were stacked by the sink, and his clothes littered the floor. His bed was rumpled, as if he wasn't sleeping well. She decided to ignore the mess.

Instead she set the shopping bags on the table. "Here are the items you needed. Clarinda was busy, and asked me to bring them over."

He lifted those tired eyebrows in question but didn't say anything.

"So where do you want me to put the food?" Her voice trailed away as she looked at the items filling the single shelf devoted to food storage. She'd had enough. She'd clean the dishes and organize the space before she did anything else.

Of course the stove wasn't lit. During summer heat, who would light it except for cooking? Sighing, she stepped outside to gather some kindling and started the fire so she could heat dishwater.

"You don't have to do that." Wallace's voice sounded muffled as he checked out the food bags. "Mmm, these muffins are good."

Mary Anne smiled. She had baked the muffins herself. "There's fresh butter in there, too. Go ahead, eat what you want. The dishes shouldn't take too long." *I hope.*

He ate the muffin and munched on cantaloupe. "As long as you're here." He coughed, as if a seed had gone done his throat, and, after a deep breath, coughed again. Mary Anne poured him a cup of water, and he drank it deeply.

More than a seed was causing the cough. "Spit it out."

"I would love for you to look at the manuscript." The words rushed from his mouth. Having gotten out that much, he slowed down. "I need someone to proofread it for me. You know the material better than anyone else. You're the perfect one to help me, if you're willing…"

Mary Anne froze behind the sink as the meaning of his words sank in. *Act natural.* Her mouth hurt as she forced it into a smile. Instead of answering, she took her time stacking the dishes.

"Well, what do you say?"

More than anything, Mary Anne wanted to give him the answer he wanted. "Doesn't the publisher do that for you?" The shriveled skin on her dishwater hands only reflected what she felt on the inside.

"Not exactly. But don't worry. I can go over it myself."

She turned around, but he had buried his nose in the shopping bags again.

"What are these doing here?" Wallace pulled out the colored pencils she had chosen with such care. "Where are my regular pencils?" He emptied the bag, but she knew he wouldn't find what he wanted. "These colors are great, but the editor told me he couldn't use colored sketches in the book. He asked me to redo them in pencil. I'm sure I told Clarinda that." Rifling through the bag again, he found the shopping list where it rested on the bottom.

Mary Anne grabbed the edge of the sink, willing her wilting legs to keep her upright.

"No, she wrote down No. 2 pencils. Why did you buy me colored pencils instead?" He sounded more curious than annoyed.

Her legs gave up the battle, and she started to collapse.

Wallace hurried around the table to prevent Mary Anne from falling and helped her to the chair. "Darling, what's wrong?" The endearment slipped out, but he didn't care.

She opened her eyes, blue darkened almost to midnight with confusion, and her mouth opened in a small O. "I.... fainted?"

He nodded. "Do you want to lie down while I fetch Dr. Landrum? You shouldn't have come out here if you're feeling sick."

A grimace crossed her face. "I'm not sick."

Wallace didn't believe her. "At least let me fix you some tea." The water in the kettle came to a quick boil. She sat without speaking, hardly moving.

"A muffin, maybe?" He handed one to her before stirring sugar into the tea.

She ate the muffin one slow bite at a time. Color returned to her face but the haunted look stayed firmly in place.

"What is troubling you? Don't worry about the pencils.

I'll get some the next time I go to town." He smiled. "The colors you chose were a perfect match."

"Oh, Wallace." Tears came to her eyes. "You don't understand." She took the shopping list and held it, upside down.

An improbable suspicion forced itself into Wallace's mind. It couldn't be. But it explained her strange behavior today. He settled into his chair, examining his hypothesis from different angles. Mary Anne's intelligence had made itself clear. But this other...was it possible?

The possibilities running through Wallace's mind kept him rooted to his chair for long minutes. Every one of the endangered birds they had observed could have flown through the windows without him noticing. Noises, sights, smells, all sank from his consciousness as he sat lost in thought.

Until one unexpected, unwanted sound intruded. A soft voice said, "I'm so sorry." The door whispered open and closed. As soon as Mary Anne left, Wallace felt her absence, and he came to full alert.

She had brought him food and washed his dishes, taking care of his needs. In return, he had ignored her pain, her embarrassment. He hadn't even thanked her for coming to the cabin with food and supplies. He stared at the paper ready for him to slip into the typewriter, ready for a start on the next page. The book would have to wait.

Whether he should seek out Aunt Flo or Mary Anne, he couldn't decide. After packing a few things in an overnight bag, he headed out the door. When he reached the road, God would have to guide him to town or to the farm.

As he neared the cemetery, he heard the sound of soft weeping, and his decision was made. He sped up his steps and jumped over the fence into the graveyard.

Mary Anne huddled in front of a granite stone. Her fingers ran over the letters etched into the face of the marker. She traced it, twice, without looking at him. "I think that's a C."

"It is." Wallace perched beside her. "My grandmother, Clara Farley Tuttle. Born March 1, 1840. Died September 18, 1924. She was a feisty lady to the very end."

She twisted around, pulling her knees toward her chest. "I should have told you before. That I can't read."

Wallace shook his head. "Why should you? I made assumptions, that's all."

She dug her fingers into the grass, as if ready to rip it up by the roots. Tension screamed from her bunched fingers, the way she held on to the slender blades as if they held the key to her continued existence.

Her head still bent toward the ground, she said, "You don't realize how lucky you have it. Your grandmother started a school. All of you are teachers or went to college or read the latest books…You're all so much smarter than I am."

"Absolutely not." The words burst from Wallace. "It's true, our family treasures book learning. But I have watched you all this summer. You absorb information like a sponge, turning into an encyclopedia of knowledge. I don't know anyone who can quote scripture the way you can, not even our pastor. And the way you understand the birds." He pointed to a V of geese heading south overhead. "I thought you were taking books home and studying up on birds at night."

"You're a good teacher."

He snorted. "It has little to do with me and everything to do with what you taught yourself, just by observing the birds and their habits. You noticed everything—what they eat, where they live, even which parent does what with the eggs. A lot of what I'm putting in the book are things you showed me."

She hugged her knees to her chest and lowered her head into the circle of her arms. "You're just saying that to make me feel better." The words came out muffled.

Wallace had spent enough time around women to know

there were some arguments no amount of logic could win. This was one of them. *Help, Lord.* The Holy Ghost understood the things her heart couldn't put into words. Maybe He'd give Wallace some insight.

Wallace couldn't imagine a child growing up without learning how to read. If she couldn't go to school, why didn't her father teach her at home? Maybe he couldn't read, either. The opposite was true in his family. The family Bible held a century and a half of births, marriages and deaths, testifying to literacy back to his earliest American ancestors. "I'm sorry." That seemed like a safe place to start.

"It's too late for me now." Tears robbed her words of clarity. "I won't go and sit with a class of children Arthur's age."

"I wouldn't either, if that was the only choice. But I have an idea. You know about the seminary, of course."

Her laughter was forced. "The one every female member of the Tuttle family has attended for the past sixty years? That your grandmother founded? I've seen the school, almost the biggest place in town."

"Grandma Clara inherited the house from her grandfather, the town banker. He thought bigger was better, and Grandma thought it was the perfect place for a school." His mind seized upon an idea. "It's so big, it's nearly impossible to keep up with the housework. During the school year, the students do regular chores, but over the summer it's different." He snapped his fingers. "In fact, right now Aunt Flo's making herself crazy, getting everything ready for the new school year. She could use an extra pair of hands to help."

"Sure, I'd be happy to help." Again, that rueful laugh. "At least I've learned how to clean."

Wallace winced at the bitterness in her voice. Did she see herself as someone destined to nothing higher than cleaning other people's messes? With a rush, he remembered his rude oversight. *Good going, Tuttle.* "I'll say. You did an amazing job back in my cabin. I don't think the dishes were that clean when I moved in."

A smile flickered around her mouth.

"And I should have spoken up while you were still there, but when I realized how blind I had been, I was speechless." Was Aunt Flo the answer? He hoped so. "Aunt Flo can be a bit of a martinet. But she's good at heart. And she's a grand teacher."

Mary Anne sank back a little at those words.

He rushed on. "Only if you're interested, of course. But you've got two weeks before school starts. At the rate you learn, you might be ready to tackle Shakespeare by then."

She tucked her knees underneath and pushed up from the ground. "Very well. If your aunt is ready to take on a student my age, I'm willing to learn."

Chapter 14

By Monday morning after her discussion with Wallace, Mary Anne had moved into the female seminary. Eager to start her new adventure, she woke up early on the first day. She stretched her arms over her head and kicked her legs against the bed with childlike abandon. Working, *living,* at a school earning cash money and, God be praised, learning how to read at long last.

Not that Mary Anne needed money, except as an excuse for having money to spend. The Tuttles probably knew she had money, from the way Winnie had commented on the cost of her Victoria coupe. Reluctantly, Mary Anne had left the car at the farm. She didn't expect anyone from New York to search for her in this town, but the coupe was as good as a lighthouse for attracting attention. She needed to trade it in for something less conspicuous before she started driving again.

She'd give the Tuttles every penny she had to be able to

read. Only, as with the times she had offered payment for truck repairs and room and board, they had turned her down. When she persisted, Clarinda said something about learning how to receive being harder than learning how to give.

As far as Mary Anne could see, the Tuttles had never had much experience in learning how to receive, either. They excelled in giving, however.

For now, she'd let them. Someday, when she was far away, she'd send a check or something.

Far away. Mary Anne needed to leave this fall, before the first snowfall. If she didn't, she'd be stuck in Vermont through winter. In that case, she didn't know if she would ever work up the courage to leave.

Outside the window, the sky turned gray. A glance at the clock revealed the hour: six o'clock. Even before she could read the numbers, she had learned how to tell time by the position of the hands on the dial.

Six was a good hour to get up. She put on blue jeans. She didn't think Aunt Flo would object, since today was a work day. Shaking her head, she knew she wouldn't find it so easy to decide what to wear if she expected to see Wallace today.

After a brief knock, Florence Tuttle came in. She'd invited Mary Anne to call her "Aunt Flo," but Mary Anne felt uncomfortable using the title when she was working for her. With a backbone as stiff as a grave marker, and hair as prickly as a hedge hog, dressed in clothes about a decade out of style, glasses perched on her nose, Miss Tuttle looked like the perfect school matron.

Winnie complained about her sometimes, but Clarinda said she was only as stern as she needed to be. She reminded Mary Anne of President Theodore Roosevelt when he said to "speak softly and carry a big stick. You will go far." "Aunt Flo" would work in private, Mary Anne decided, but she'd call her "Miss Tuttle" in front of the students. Right now she looked like a Miss Tuttle, pursing her lips as she considered Mary Anne's attire. "Blue jeans." She said it like a pejorative, as if she had never seen a woman in blue jeans before or, if she did, the trousers put the lady in the same unflattering category as flappers.

"I thought since I was cleaning…" Mary Anne jumped to the closet and reached for one of her darker skirts. "But I can change in a snap."

Aunt Flo shook a finger at her. "Your choice of clothing does not concern me, except when it reflects on the seminary. Let me see." She studied the clothes hanging in the wardrobe. "Hmm, you have good taste in clothes."

Thanks to Clarinda.

The administrator pulled out the dress that had belonged to Mary Anne's mother. "This one suits you well."

Mary Anne nodded.

"I think it best if you have clothing similar to what the students wear. I usually wear dark-colored skirts myself, similar to the blue wool jersey you have hanging here. I see you have black as well. Perhaps a dark green and another one in brown, as well." Aunt Flo went through her blouses, setting aside ones of neutral, mostly *boring* colors. "These will do. Our girls wear jumpers made of dark blues and greens, like the mountains Vermont is known for, with white blouses. Of course, when you go to church or into town, you may choose something different to wear."

That was a reasonable request. Mary Anne had worn a uniform before, back when she worked as a waitress. "I'll get fabric for the skirts on Saturday morning."

Aunt Flo started to speak—to offer to pay for the skirts, Mary Anne guessed—then hesitated. "If you like, you can take the afternoon to go shopping."

"I'd appreciate that."

"Very well. This morning I will show you the rooms that

need to be freshened before school opens. After you return from your shopping, we can begin your studies, if you wish."

Mary Anne's heart about jumped out of her chest. *Studies.* What a fancy word to use about teaching a grown woman her ABCs. What if she discovered she was too old to learn, after all? "I'd like that."

After a hearty breakfast, Aunt Flo took Mary Anne to the second floor. "We need these rooms cleaned first. Our teachers will be arriving early next week, so we want to be prepared for them."

Teachers. Of course. "How many people are on your staff?" The house was empty except for the two of them.

"Did you think I run the place all by myself?" Aunt Flo huffed, a sound that matched her prim exterior. "We have five professors, including myself, but they have the summer off, and the cook and her husband."

"How many students?"

"We have two dozen girls who are completing their secondary education, and two dozen more who attend classes to prepare for entrance to the university. Several of our graduates have received advanced placement in college after their time here." Pride rang in Aunt Flo's voice.

So many years of school. It seemed like children would have learned all there was to learn by eighth grade, and these women attended classes for twelve years and more. Mary Anne couldn't imagine it.

Maybe after her first lesson today, she'd get so excited about it that she'd still be studying fourteen years later.

Wallace rolled the last sheet of typing paper out of his typewriter. He had met his goal: to finish typing the manuscript by the end of August. The birds of Vermont were Wallace's love, but this book was his labor. He didn't know if he'd ever want to try it again.

He had inserted blank pages where he wanted to include sketches of the birds. His book included nine endangered birds, but he wanted to include more pictures than that.

Over the course of the spring and summer, he had filled four sketchbooks with pictures. He glanced at the wall, where Mary Anne's picture of the titwillow hung. If she would let him, he'd include it in the book as a way to thank her. She wouldn't appreciate it, though.

He picked up a new yellow pencil and sharpened with a mechanical sharpener that had become popular about the time he started school. His father told him he was lucky he didn't have to whittle the wood with his pen knife. For school work, he kept his pencils as sharp as possible, but for sketching, he needed different thicknesses of lead. In addition to the different grades of pencils he bought at the store, he had used his Swiss army knife to pare others as needed. The sharpener worked well for the No. 2 pencils. He cranked it through until the lead was so thin it broke, and he had to work the machine again. *There.* The lightest touch of a pencil could suggest the wispy white feathers around the bald eagle's neck. Searching through his set of pencils, he chose one to suggest dashes of color among the bird's feathers.

The memory of the dismay on Mary Anne's face when he asked her about the colored pencils she had picked with obvious care shook him. He wished he could convince the publisher to use color.

The publisher said no one would buy such an expensive book. Would anyone buy it, no matter what the cost, aside from a few Audubon enthusiasts? The editor suggested offering the colored sketches as prints, but Wallace doubted anyone would be interested.

His enthusiasm for the book disappeared along with Mary Anne.

Without her, he might never finish *Endangered Birds of Northern Vermont*.

Chapter 15

When Aunt Flo first used the fourteenth chapter of Exodus as practice reading material, Mary Anne couldn't understand why she gave her such challenging verses. Next she asked Mary Anne to put the chapter into her own words. Aside from spelling, that wasn't hard. She knew the story well from Sunday school, and all she had to do was to add information not usually mentioned in children's classes.

After that session, Aunt Flo laid down a challenge. "The seminary's annual scripture contest is coming up in two weeks, on October 16."

"Yes, of course." Mary Anne nodded. The girls had talked about little else since the beginning of the school year. Winning brought great prestige with it.

"Of course I want to see you take part in the memory contest. Our townspeople will find your retention of God's Word as inspiring as I do, I'm sure."

Mary Anne fidgeted a little. "But I don't attend the seminary."

Aunt Flo waved her concern away. "I have an even greater challenge for you. I want you to read, too, and the chapter you just read is the assigned passage."

Read? Mary Anne would have laughed out loud if not for the serious expression on Aunt Flo's face.

They practiced it again the next night, and the next, every day for a week, reading the verses out of order, probing into the feelings of Moses and the Israelites.

Mary Anne loved the story of crossing the Red Sea, once she got past place names like Pihahiroth and Baalzephon and unusual verbs like spake and encamp. As Mary Anne read, she felt as if she was acting out all the scenes and lines. Aunt Flo had warned her against memorizing the verses, but Mary Anne decided the rule didn't apply to memorizing the pronunciations. She prayed she made it from beginning to end without stumbling too badly.

By the end of the last session, Aunt Flo said, "You'll do." A giveaway twinkle in her eyes indicated her silent approval. She pushed her glasses back up her nose and closed her Bible. "You do know, of course, that since I am one of the judges, I will expect more from you. No one else has private tutoring sessions." Aunt Flo used her iron voice.

Now competition Sunday had arrived. Mary Anne took her place between students and professors, her family Bible clutched tight in her hands.

Wallace sat with the family in their pew at the Maple Notch Community Church. On the second Sunday of October, the church hosted the annual scripture reading and memory contest sponsored by the seminary.

"You'll be glad you came. You might be surprised at what you see." Winnie had winked at him with her remark. Did she expect to win? She was bright enough, but she didn't share Aunt Flo's passion for academics. If participation wasn't required of all students, Winnie might not take part.

Competition Sunday had evolved into an all-day event over the years. A community dinner followed morning worship. The competition began after the meal and continued until both winners were declared, with a break for the evening meal if necessary.

The organist began playing "Lead On, O King Eternal." The back door opened, and the congregation stood to watch the processional. The girls came in two by two, wearing matching jumpers of blue and green plaid with white cotton blouses. Winnie had added a red ribbon to her dark hair to set herself apart. Behind the students came the teachers.

Aunt Flo and Mary Anne marched at the end of the line. *Mary Anne?* Wallace's mind raced with possibilities. Even with her hair in a brown bun and wearing a simple blue skirt and white sweater, she stood out like a blue jay among a flock of sparrows. She sailed past the family pew without a single glance in his direction, but he dared to dream that the heightened color in her cheeks indicated her awareness of him.

After the girls sat in the choir rows, Aunt Flo stood behind the pulpit. After a few words of introduction, she explained the format for the competition. "The memory contest works much like a spelling bee. The first time a girl is unable to complete a verse, she sits. The last one standing from each class is the winner of that division. The last one standing in the competition wins the overall title."

As the girls formed lines at the front of the platform, Flo continued speaking. "This year we are privileged to have a unique competitor. Although this woman is not a student, she has agreed to take part. She will join the competition on an equal level with our students. Please join me in welcoming Miss Mary Anne Laurents."

Wallace couldn't restrain the grin that spread across his face. He wanted to stand and cheer. Instead, he joined in the enthusiastic clapping. She'd win; the other girls didn't stand a chance.

One of the first year students stuttered so badly Aunt Flo invited her to sit. She looked grateful as she ran back to her chair, but she'd improve by next year. Aunt Flo would see to it.

Winnie's spot came at the end of the second-year students. "'Surely goodness and mercy shall follow me all the days of my life: and I will dwell in the house of the Lord forever.'" She finished the psalm her class had quoted verse by verse. Each class recited a different passage, a verse at a time.

After Winnie, Wallace had to wait through three dozen more girls before Mary Anne's turn came. A serious expression on her face, she started with the reference. "Romans 8:1."

Mary Anne was glad she came after the girls who were preparing for university. She was close to them in age, but she would have been embarrassed to stand with the girls younger than Winnie.

The first time through lasted a long time. What if she became nervous and forgot a word? By the third time through, three girls had returned to their seats. As the sixth round started, the girls were asked to quote two verses at a time. "'For to be carnally minded is death…'"

Over the next five rounds, the group cut in half. After ten rounds, they were asked to quote three verses. "'The Spirit itself beareth witness…'" After that, the numbers quickly dwindled. By the time Mary Anne reached the last three verses of the chapter, only one competitor remained. "'…shall be able to separate us from the love of God which is in Christ Jesus our Lord.'" Mary Anne repeated the words with great conviction. If she hadn't known the truth of that statement before she came to Maple Notch, she knew it now.

Her one remaining competitor, Shirley Baston, a post-secondary school student destined for the mission field, turned to verses from the tenth chapter of Romans. "How shall they believe in him of whom they have not heard?" She finished the passage with a flourish, her feet bouncing like the beautiful feet Paul described. Her smile held a hint of triumph when she looked at Mary Anne.

If Shirley thought Mary Anne couldn't continue with Romans 9 after finishing the previous chapter, she was wrong. "'I say the truth in Christ, I lie not…'"

Mary Anne thought she heard a cricket chirping in the silence that greeted her recitation. Spontaneous clapping broke out across the congregation, and Wallace surged to his feet. Heat flaming in her cheeks, she took her spot behind Shirley, who clapped along with the rest. Leaning forward, she said in a low voice no one else could hear, "Well done. I will not compete with a woman so blessed of the Lord."

Shirley shook Mary Anne's hand, gestured for Aunt Flo to join them and took her place behind the pulpit. The congregation quieted down. "I concede the competition to this amazing woman of God. May she continue to bless the people of Maple Notch for many years to come."

That brought the room to their feet again, and Aunt Flo shook Mary Anne's hand. "Congratulations." She handed Mary Anne a slender, soft calf leather-bound Bible she had spied in the office yesterday. "We will have your name stenciled on the cover, now that we know who the winner is. I hope you will honor us by reading from this copy of God's Word in the upcoming competition."

Taking the Bible in her hands, Mary Anne fled to her seat next to the teachers, wondering how she would handle the next battle. Reading a few words from the story of Moses and the Red Sea might seem easy to some folks, compared to quoting chapters of the Bible, but not for Mary Anne. Never for her.

Once again, Aunt Flo explained the rules. For this competition, the professors competed against each other. Each woman would read the same passage of scripture. The pastor and Clarinda, both trustees of the school, along with Aunt Flo, would judge the reading based on accuracy, clarity and expression.

Mary Anne listened to the readers with interest. Mademoiselle DePaul read with a distinct French accent that hindered Mary Anne from understanding some of the words. Her pronunciation was off, but she read with a flourish that made the chapter fun.

The gymnasium instructor, Miss Barber, read the verses in her straightforward manner, each word clearly enunciated but about as exciting as her lectures on girls' health.

Mary Anne's stomach twisted as her turn approached. Aunt Flo had placed the silk bookmark at the correct place and she breathed a silent thanks. She didn't want to fumble through the Bible as if she didn't know her way around. Looking across the audience, she took comfort from the smiles and expectant looks on faces. A beaming Wallace leaned forward, eager to hear her.

She swallowed. She couldn't let down the people who counted on her. Aunt Flo—the Lord—*Wallace*. What would it be like to read the Bible together someday? To their children?

Heat rushed into her cheeks. Let the congregation think her nervousness caused it. Before long, the exciting story of God's miraculous deliverance caught her in the narrative and bubbled in her voice. Oh, to have been a fish in that wall of water on either side of dry land as the people of Israel walked through. Whenever she read about the waves crashing over Pharaoh and his chariots, her voice dropped.

By the time she reached the end of the chapter, she couldn't tell if she had mixed up any words or said them wrong. The story had carried her along.

Catching her breath, she dared to look at Wallace, who nodded, a private message between the two of them. She closed her Bible, said "Amen," and returned to her chair.

Wallace raised half out of his seat before Clarinda tugged him back down. "Don't embarrass her," she whispered.

If he hadn't heard Mary Anne's awkward reading of the last Elson Reader primer after a single week of lessons, he never would have believed it possible. Even now, he could scarcely believe his ears. She read from Exodus as if she was a Shakespearean actress.

Restraining his enthusiasm, Wallace paid attention to the final three readers. Two of the teachers read with some skill, but only the English teacher came close to matching Mary Anne's rendition. Her first year as a teacher came during Wallace's last year of high school, and she had won the contest every year since.

After everyone finished, the audience stood and clapped. The teacher waited in line, Mary Anne with them, her head bowed modestly, the new Bible clutched in her hands. Aunt Flo invited them to sit while the judges conferred.

As far as Wallace was concerned, Mary Anne should win the competition, but he acknowledged his prejudice. A couple of mispronounced words would count against her, but he didn't understand the judging system. The audience grew restless while the three judges lingered over reaching a decision. Murmured conversations took over the sanctuary.

Clarinda touched Wallace on the arm, an understanding smile lighting her face. She nodded in the direction of Wallace's gaze—Mary Anne. He braced himself for some teasing comment.

"She did very well." The pride in Clarinda's voice echoed his feelings.

Wallace crossed his arms on his chest. "You knew she couldn't read?"

Chapter 16

Clarinda nodded. Yes, she knew the truth about Mary Anne's reading ability.

Was Wallace the only person blind to Mary Anne's handicap when she arrived?

Clarinda didn't have a chance to say any more before Aunt Flo took her place behind the pulpit. "Before I announce the winner, let us celebrate all of the readers for an excellent job." She brought her hands together, bringing everyone in the sanctuary to their feet again.

After they returned to their seats, Aunt Flo spoke again. "And the winner this year is Miss Emmaline Garrett."

The smile drained from Wallace's face. He had so hoped Mary Anne would win. Clarinda shook her head.

Instead of heading for the pulpit, Miss Garrett approached Mary Anne. When she shook her head, the English professor insisted. *Go, Mary Anne, go.*

He thought he had said the words silently but Winnie and Howie took up the chant. "Go, Mary Anne, go."

The audience joined the chant, clapping in rhythm until Mary Anne took her place at the pulpit with Miss Garrett.

The tall teacher silenced the room as easily as she settled her classroom. "I appreciate the honor the judges have given me in choosing me as the winner of the Bible reading competition. I am always thrilled to share God's Word to the best of my ability. But today, another deserves a share in the award."

She brought Mary Anne forward. "Miss Laurents, I want you to accept the award on our behalf this year."

Aunt Flo came up on Mary Anne's other side. "Miss Garrett, thank you for your generosity of spirit. You are the quality of Christian woman our students strive to become."

More applause broke out at that remark.

Aunt Flo presented a small statue—Wallace had seen its duplicate many times, an open Bible in the arms of a woman seated on a chair—and a wrapped gift that could only be a book. "I cannot think of anyone who will enjoy this more, or gain more benefit from it." She embraced Mary Anne, the audience applauded a final time, and the competition had ended for another year.

The night after the competition, Mary Anne dressed in her finest dress instead of the uniform-like outfits she wore at school. In celebration of her double win in yesterday's competition, Wallace was taking her to a local restaurant.

She picked up the statue and examined the inscription: "Best Reader, Maple Notch Female Seminary, 1927." Open in front of the statue lay her new Bible. She read the handwritten inscription at the presentation page: To Mary Anne Laurents from Florence Tuttle on behalf of Maple Notch Female Seminary.

Laurents. If only she hadn't won under false pretenses.

She wasn't Mary Anne Laurents, but how could she explain that now? Did the danger still exist? In less than a week, she would celebrate six months in Maple Notch. Even her pursuers' memory wouldn't last that long.

That small cloud didn't overshadow her pride and accomplishment—not to mention the friendship of a good man.

She looked in the mirror, pulling a curl over her forehead to relieve the severe bun she wore during the day, and fiddled with her hair until someone knocked on her door.

Aunt Flo let herself in. "He's here."

Of course tonight's dinner with Wallace would create a sensation among the girls. Even with her outsider's position, neither staff nor student, she heard everything that came through the rumor mill. She didn't hold any illusions about her own privacy.

"Perhaps the back stairs?" Aunt Flo suggested. Mary Anne followed her down the twisting steps. At least the narrow steps would keep a dozen pairs of eyes from following her with keen interest.

Wallace waited for her in the front room, fedora in hand, looking at the pictures of his ancestors. Mary Anne enjoyed the picture of Clara Farley Tuttle the most. She must have been a formidable woman, to start a school for girls in 1864. But her eyes twinkled behind her glasses and her face radiated contentment.

Wallace had the same gentle gray eyes, but despite the scholar's glasses, he retained the solid musculature of his farmer forbears. He was a man comfortable in the open fields or in a classroom, on the factory floor or in the office. A man headed places. And he had asked her out to dinner.

Smiling, he stretched out his hands and took hers. "Let me look at you."

Her cheeks burned as he studied her.

"Something looks different today." His eyes twinkled a

bit more. "It must be those two awards you won last night. Success becomes you."

She twisted to brush away the compliment, but he tightened his grip on her hands. "I mean it. Have you read your story in today's paper?"

Newspaper? A memory of a flashing light and a man's pen poised over a notebook darted through Mary Anne's brain. "No."

"Doesn't surprise me. Aunt Flo only likes papers that carry national news, not our local *Gazette,* so I bought extra copies. I'll take one with us to the restaurant and leave the rest here."

He draped her shawl over her shoulders—this late in September, the evenings often turned quite cold—and led her into the crisp evening air. "We could drive, but I thought you might enjoy a walk under the canopy of God's artwork."

Mary Anne nodded. She had never seen so many trees in one place, all changing color, vivid reds and oranges and golds. Out in the forest, the sight must be glorious. "Do the birds migrate?"

"Not many, no. The geese fly farther south, of course. I always look forward to their return in the spring."

Upon their arrival at the restaurant, Mary Anne's mouth watered for homey fare, and she settled on a meat loaf sandwich with mashed potatoes.

"You can have anything on the menu," Wallace said after the waitress wrote down his order for a T-bone steak with baked potato.

"I like meat loaf."

While they waited for the opening course, a vegetable soup, Wallace placed a single copy of the *Gazette* on the table. Above the fold, on the front page, Mary Anne's smiling face stared back at her. The headline announced, Maple Notch Newcomer Claims Both Awards.

"Go ahead, read it." He grinned at their private joke.

Mary Anne relived the experience through the reporter's impersonal words, learning details that had escaped her notice while she focused on her next turn.

"I'm sure you'll want several copies of this for your records." Wallace handed her a bag filled with extras.

Mary Anne flipped the paper over to read the caption beneath the photograph. She read her name and froze.

With this good a picture—and the same initials she had left behind in New York—she remained instantly recognizable. People in this town wouldn't knowingly betray her, but how far did the paper travel?

"Anyone who might want to hear the news?"

Mary Anne fought the urge to throw up. A better idea might be to burn every copy of the paper.

On Friday, Wallace spent the day in his attic room, putting the finishing touches on his manuscript. This weekend he intended to repeat his request for Mary Anne to edit the book. He didn't need a proofreader; Mary Anne's expertise lay in fact checking and wording.

A sharp rap sounded on his door, the kind Clarinda made when she demanded his attention. Placing the page he held aside, he stood and opened the door. "What is it?"

The first face he saw was Aunt Flo's. Her thin lips stretched in a severe line. "We need your help, Wallace."

Aunt Flo only called him Wallace when she was seriously upset. His heart tripped. "What is it?"

"Mary Anne has left town, that's what happened. She's cleared out all of her things, both here and at the seminary."

Wallace turned his attention to Clarinda. She nodded. "She came by here for her car."

Wallace dashed down the stairs and out the door without waiting for the women to follow. The dark recesses of the barn shouted the truth of their disclosure. The glorious

Victoria Coupe, which Mary Anne had arrived in, had disappeared. How had he missed the noise of the car engine starting while he was working in the attic?

He ran back to the house, ready to check her room. The two women waited at the bottom of the stairs.

"Is everything gone?" The words forced themselves out of his dry throat.

"Both here and at the school. Her suitcases, her old clothes, her new clothes, even her books." Aunt Flo's clipped voice stripped away any remaining hope.

"She left this." Clarinda handed him an envelope. "It's addressed to you, so I haven't read it." She squeezed past Wallace. "But let's go to the kitchen while you read it. I suspect we can all use a bracing cup of coffee."

A bracing cup of coffee sounded right. No sweet tea could soften this news.

He opened the letter, written on lined paper. Several crossed out words and ink smears indicated her agitation as she wrote—otherwise she would have taken the time to figure out the correct spelling and prepare a clean copy.

He told himself to expect the worst. What had she hidden that she didn't think he would understand? *Maybe she's married. Somewhere she has a family she abandoned.* That didn't fit the Mary Anne he knew, but what had compelled her to disappear without warning?

"Go ahead and read it. I'm sure she wouldn't leave without a good reason." Aunt Flo tapped the paper. "You can share with us whatever you feel is appropriate."

Enough with the rationalizations. He read silently, in case she had included any personal message.

I'm not who I claimed to be. I ran into someone from my past, and he poses a real threat, not only to me but to people I hold dear. I don't dare stay here in Maple Notch for fear he will harm you in his pursuit of me. You asked me once where

I was headed when I ran into your car on the bridge. I was on the run, getting as far away from New York as possible. I should have continued on my way a long time ago, but I grew comfortable with you and your family.

Wallace forced himself to continue reading.

I am so sorry. You have all been so kind to me, and Wallace, I have come to care for you more than I should. I have allowed my feelings to overcome my better judgment. Only God knows if we shall ever meet again.

Tears formed in Wallace's eyes, and Clarinda laid a soft hand on his shoulder. "We all care for her, Wallace. This is hard for us all."

Nodding, he shared all the news, all except the last bit.

"She's not who she said she was. After living with someone as long as she was with us, I feel like I know her well. I know who she *is,* although the details may have changed. Like her hair." Clarinda poured freshly brewed coffee into mugs and handed one to each of them.

"But where would she have run into someone from her past? And whom?"

"The newspaper." Now Mary Anne's hesitation made more sense. "It included her picture and name and even where she's been living. She paled when I suggested sending a copy to people she might have known in New York. Perhaps the wrong person got ahold of a copy and came up here to find her."

"The poor child." Clarinda shook her head before blowing on the steaming coffee.

Wallace wanted to jump into his truck and chase after her. "Do you know when she left?"

Clarinda shrugged. "She told Aunt Flo she wanted to take the car out for a spin herself, and that she wanted to see the fall leaves."

The kind of trip Wallace had planned for them.

"She even said she might spend the night on the road, since it was the weekend, and not to worry about her. It was a little odd, but I didn't think anything of it until Aunt Flo arrived here with the letter."

So, she had a head start of several hours, in a car faster than his truck, headed to an unknown destination. "What can we do?" He ached to pursue her, but knew the futility of it.

"We pray." Aunt Flo spoke with straightforward authority.

Times like this, prayer never seemed like enough.

Chapter 17

Mary Anne handed cash to the hotel clerk on a back street in Montreal. Thank God she had found a place with English-speaking employees that accepted American money. The question of a different currency hadn't occurred to her as she prepared for flight.

The trip to Montreal hadn't taken nearly as long as Mary Anne had feared. Driving through until she arrived at the small boardinghouse on the outskirts of the city, rather than making frequent stops, had sped her on her way.

"Comment vous appelez-vous?" The petite brunette's face expressed the universal expression of polite inquiry.

"I only speak English," Mary Anne said. Perhaps she should push herself to continue on to Ottawa, where English was the primary language.

"English? Of course. What is your name, mademoiselle?"

"Mary Anne." She hesitated and then added, "Lamont."

"Bon." After they completed the check-in, the clerk es-

corted her to a comfortable room and handed Mary Anne a sheet of paper. "This is our menu in English, for your convenience."

Mary Anne ordered the first item on the menu, some kind of fish, and asked for a cup of *café au lait*. Although she had never drunk it, it sounded deliciously decadent. While she waited for the food, she stared out the window at the narrow street in front of the house. Her coupe took up a large part of the converted carriage house behind the building. If not for that, she didn't know where she would have parked her car. Tomorrow, she'd go to Ottawa, or even farther, far enough away that she could relax for a few days.

She took out her new Bible, inscribed with her alias. After giving consideration to leaving it behind, wanting to forget the web of lies she had spun while in Maple Notch, she decided against it. It meant too much to her, as well as the book of Shakespeare's sonnets for winning the reading competition. Less than a week had passed. How could something so good turn into the occasion of her discovery?

Aunt Flo had used a couple of sonnets for reading material. "Shall I compare thee to a summer's day? Thou art more lovely and more temperate." Rhyme and rhythm made the old-fashioned words easier to read, and each line reminded her of Wallace. Now that she had left him behind, she didn't know if she would choose to struggle through any more of the poems.

But Shakespeare was a master. She'd rather wrestle with his words than worry about the man she'd spotted at the store. The man with cold blue eyes and impossibly black hair had killed her father and then discovered he'd had a witness.

After she had spotted him, she'd backed out of the store without drawing any attention to herself. She rushed back to the school, stuffed everything into her suitcases and headed out of town as soon as she picked up her car. Leafing through the book of sonnets, Mary Anne found one that started "When, in disgrace with fortune." Disgrace, she understood, and lately she felt like fortune had forsaken her. She continued reading until she encountered a strange word, breaking it down the way Aunt Flo had taught her. *Be,* followed by *weep. Beweep.* A fancy way to say he was crying.

The food arrived, and Mary Anne decided she liked the fish sauce, as well as the flaky roll that melted in her mouth. She might even enjoy this trip if…if she wasn't all alone, beweeping, an outcast as Shakespeare had put it.

Although she made each bite last as long as possible, the food disappeared quickly. By now, the folks in Maple Notch knew she had left. Were they worried? Disappointed? Angry? Any of those, or all, made sense.

Oh, Wallace. He had given her so much, and she had betrayed his trust with lies and deceit. Even if she wanted to go back, she couldn't, not unless she was willing to face all the lies she had told.

After dinner, bubbling foam helped soak out the day's aches. As she lay in the water, scrubbing her skin as if she could remove fear and self-loathing with the sponge, she realized she had never asked for forgiveness from the One who promised it. How could she expect God to direct her paths when she had unconfessed sins in her life?

Right then and there, she prayed. "And tomorrow, Lord? Give me a clear sign about where You are directing my steps."

With that, she climbed onto the high mattress under warm comforters and rested. After a hard night's sleep, she awoke early, before the day had quite dawned.

Shortly after Mary Anne rang her bell, the hotel clerk appeared, bearing a cup of hot coffee, perfect for clearing the dregs of sleep from her mind. Eager to start the day, she

read her Bible, begging God for guidance, but nothing crys-
tallized in her mind.

She had to make a start, and the map seemed like a good
place. Yesterday she couldn't make sense out of it, but perhaps when she spread it out on the table so she could see it
all at once, she would understand it better.

The clerk at the gas stop had marked her starting point as
well as several nearby cities. Mary Anne asked for the loca-
tion of several places, in New York and New Hampshire as
well as Canada, to confuse possible pursuers.

She took a piece of paper and used its edge to draw straight
lines between stars. Now to choose her destination. She put
her thumb at the star that represented Montreal. "Lord, show
me where." Closing her eyes, she let her fingers wander
around the map. When she opened her eyes, her pointer finger had stuck at a town just south of the place she purchased
gas: Maple Notch. *God, this isn't funny.*

Still uncertain, she packed her bags and went to the front
desk to check out. The desk clerk, a more matronly version
of the young woman who had greeted her last night, smiled
at Mary Anne's approach. "You must be the mademoiselle
my daughter told me about last night. How lovely you were,
how brave you were to travel all alone…" The woman continued babbling, and Mary Anne wondered if she would be
so noticeable everywhere she traveled. Was there nowhere
she could go and remain unnoticed?

She chatted longer than she wished to out of politeness
before leaving the hotel. As she turned the coupe onto the
street, she studied the choices before her. East or west? North
or south?

The map pointed to Maple Notch. Mary Anne chewed on
a fingernail. Was it possible that leaving Maple Notch would
create the notice she wanted to avoid? People might comment
if she missed church and school, a mere week after creating

such a public splash. Her attempt to escape detection might instead send her pursuers on her trail.

God, show me if I'm wrong. She turned south, heading back toward Maple Notch, praying the Tuttle family would welcome her back into their embrace. Her fingernail tore away, ripping a bit of skin in the process. She deserved the pain. Steeling her backbone for a rough road and an even rougher reception upon her return, she took the winding road at a tourist's pace.

Saturday morning Wallace awoke to his new reality. Mary Anne was gone. Permanently. He escaped to his refuge to give his heart time to heal. The cabin would keep him warm for a few days and maybe weeks.

He picked a posy of asters to lay at the grave Mary Anne had claimed as her own in the family cemetery. The last time she had visited the graveyard, he had walked with her. Only a week ago, they hunted the wrens together. The male soared in the sky overhead. Of the female, they found no evidence.

As he approached the cabin, he realized he had made a foolish choice. Every inch of space carried some memory of his time with Mary Anne. He was better off in his attic sanctuary, where he could add this latest heartbreak to the other pains he had endured while pacing the floorboards.

Torn between two places certain to bring pain, Wallace remained in the one that witnessed generations of his family's deepest sorrows. The ancestor who had given his life at the second battle of Fort Ticonderoga during the Revolutionary War had christened the plot with his bravery and patriotism. Others had died from illness and wounds and old age. Among the most recent additions were his parents and Grandma Clara. If Wallace's heart stopped beating the way that it wanted to, he might take a spot next to them sooner than he should. *Nonsense, Wallace.* Having this tangible place to remember each lost loved one reminded him of Mary Anne's loss, her flight from the home where both of her parents had died.

Bunching up his fists on both sides of his head, he boxed his ears. Mary Anne, Mary Anne. He couldn't get her out of his mind. At least at the farm Clarinda would bring him an occasional cup of tea and cookies.

Him, a grown man, wanting his sister to mother him like a hurt child. He refused to do that. This afternoon he would head to the fields to help Howard with the harvest. His brother-in-law wouldn't ask questions. His silence would give Wallace a chance to wash away the pain in his heart.

That decided, he headed back down the path toward home. As he neared the road, he heard the purring of a motor that sounded like the coupe's engine once Mary Anne had tinkered with it.

He was in bad shape if even the sound of a car reminded him of Mary Anne. A car rounded the bend, the shiny blue that sparkled better than a clear night. The driver of the car had gleaming brown hair...

It couldn't be.

It was.

Mary Anne had returned. He ran onto the road where she must see him, then backed out of her way. She applied the brakes and waited without moving. She looked stunned into silence, as if another accident had robbed her of her voice.

This time, he took the first step. Walking up to the passenger door, he peered in. "Welcome back, Mary Anne." *Or whatever your name might be.*

"*Bonjour,* Wallace. See, I learned at least one French word."

So she went to Quebec. He didn't know how to respond. "Has the danger...passed?"

She froze at those words. "Has anyone been asking about

me? Or possibly a—" He could see the gulp sliding down her throat. "—Marabelle Lamont?"

Marabelle Lamont. The name matched the woman who had arrived in Maple Notch. He shook his head. "Is that your real name?"

"Lamont is. Mary Anne is my given name. Marabelle was a name I picked for myself." She waved with her hands, as if dismissing the questions. "Am I welcome at the farm?"

If he wanted the answers to a dozen questions, she needed the answer to one simple request. Did she have a home to return to?

"Of course. Clarinda just got the room ready this morning." She'd been searching for clues to Mary Anne's reasons for her abrupt departure, but she didn't need to know that. He opened the door and slid into the passenger's seat. "Shall we go?"

Chapter 18

On the Friday following Mary Anne's return, Wallace was tempted to stop by Mary Anne's room but knew he would receive the same answer he had been given every day this past week: she was indisposed and didn't want company. From Clarinda, he knew Mary Ann planned to return to work at the seminary on Monday. Did she intend to speak with him before then?

She hadn't revealed any more of what had sent her rushing into the night than what she had said in her letter. Both Clarinda and Aunt Flo offered the same advice: *wait*. When she was ready to tell them—tell *him*—her story, she would. Both of them trusted her not to endanger the family.

Whenever Howard didn't need him, Wallace retraced the places he had been with Mary Anne over the past month. The restaurant owner commented on a number of strangers, but Wallace couldn't learn any more about them. They hadn't drawn attention to themselves. If they were looking for Mary Anne—or did they know her as Marabelle?—they hadn't asked for her by name.

Today Wallace made his way to the bridge where they had met for the first time. At the entrance, he pulled the truck to the side of the road, fallen leaves crunching beneath the wheels. He stared at the shadowed opening, wondering again at the brashness that had sent Mary Anne rattling across the bridge without checking for oncoming traffic. God had many reasons for making their paths cross that day, not the least of which was preserving the life of someone unaccustomed to country roads.

Buttoning his jacket, he walked onto the bridge. He didn't know what he expected to find. Long months and many cars had crossed the river since they had cleaned up the debris. Mary Anne had checked several times, making sure she had left nothing behind. He had shown her the kissing wall, had pointed out all the initials his ancestors had carved.

Come to think of it, he had done that before she could read. She had nodded and smiled as if she could identify each set of initials. What had she said? Oh, yes, that they had worn down over time, as they had.

He made his way to the center of the bridge, pausing in front of the kissing wall. Over the years, a lot of the bridge had been reconstructed. After all, more than a century had passed since it first spanned the river. Each repair job retained the kissing wall as part of the structure. The planks were now nailed onto newer wood, artwork hidden in the dark interior of the bridge. Wallace hoped generations to come would continue to record their love in this unique Maple Notch tradition.

Maybe even someday—*W.T. + M.A.L.* in a heart.

Don't be foolish. He couldn't see much of a future for them if she didn't trust him enough to tell him her whole story.

Sparkling light filtered through the cracks in the floor-boards. He walked the span, kicking the boards, assessing whether the bridge needed repair. He should ask Mary Anne her opinion. The cracks had widened since the last time he had checked, or maybe the light was stronger.

A car stopped as Wallace approached the east side of the bridge, and he stepped out of the way. As long as he had come this far, he might as well check the underside.

Beneath the bridge, the same light glittered, like coins or broken glass. Before Prohibition, wayward youths gathered to drink liquor away from their parents' watchful eyes. They'd left a lot of broken glass back then. The amount had decreased to almost nothing in the years since the eighteenth amendment took effect back in 1920.

He kept his eyes on the ground, checking for any shards of glass, but not seeing any. Once he reached the bottom of the bank, he bent his head backward to look under the floor-boards and came to a complete halt.

Large glass jars poked their heads out of wooden crates crammed into the space beneath bridge and riverbank. In fact, someone had created a false bottom, resting crates on the extra boards. Wallace peered over the top of the nearest crate. Each one of the gallon-size jugs was filled with an amber liquid.

If there was ever an occasion for righteous anger, this was it. Someone was using the Tuttle Family Bridge as a hiding place for illegal liquor.

The blood of Wallace's grandfather Daniel Tuttle, the town constable in the years following the Civil War, ran hot in Wallace's veins. The war hero, honored on a monument in the town square, had foiled a gang of bank robbers from using the Confederate raid on nearby St. Albans as a cover to rob the citizens of Maple Notch. Those robbers had used the same hiding place as these whiskey runners.

Grandpa Dan didn't let the bank robbers get away with it, and neither would Wallace, even if he was more like his schoolteacher grandmother than his heroic grandfather. The only question was *how*. He'd call for a family powwow to alert them to the danger, and then he'd bring in the police.

Mary Anne would take part in the decision-making. She might be more in danger than anyone else.

Mary Anne watched Wallace's return from her perch on the window seat in a second-floor bedroom. His quick, angry steps chopped up the ground beneath his feet. When he glanced in her direction, she lifted her hand to wave. With his arms, he gestured for her to come downstairs.

She nodded and took a soft blue sweater from the wardrobe. She ran a brush through her hair more times than necessary, wondering what was on Wallace's mind. Had he arrived ready to demand the answers due him? What could she say without putting the rest of them in danger? Did her silence protect them, or didn't they have the right to decide for themselves?

Not for the first time, she thought of Jesus's words to His disciples: "Behold, I send you forth as sheep in the midst of wolves: be ye therefore wise as serpents, and harmless as doves." Matthew 10:16, she repeated by rote and picked up her Bible in order to read the words for herself. Even before she could read, she knew Matthew was the first book in the New Testament, the first of the Gospel accounts.

She found the verse, ran her right index finger under the words, and laid the Bible on the table. How foolish she was to wonder if she was wise or harmless, a sheep or a wolf. It was time to head downstairs and meet the wolves. Or the sheep.

Everyone, including Aunt Flo, had gathered in the kitchen by the time Mary Anne joined them.

"Winnie, take the children into the parlor," Wallace said.

Winnie scowled. Mary Anne could have told him that asking a fifteen-year-old to leave an adult conversation would never work, certainly not with that sister.

Aunt Flo shook her head. "Winnie's old enough to hear this. Whatever 'this' is. Howie can take care of Betty for a few minutes."

Clarinda nodded and slipped behind the parlor door. When she returned, she looped her arm with Mary Anne's and pulled out a chair for her use.

How blessed they were. Whatever emergency troubled Wallace, he could count on his family to see him through.

How blessed she was, that they wanted her involved. Unless she was the sheep among the wolves, and they wanted to devour her.

"Let us pray." Howard's voice broke into the silence and as one, they bowed their heads. "Lord, You know what is on Wallie's mind. Grant us understanding and unity of spirit. Amen." As with most prayers she had heard from Clarinda's quiet husband, Howard kept it to the point, but captured everything that needed to be said.

Their heads rose and all eyes turned to Wallace. He cleared his throat. "I went to the old bridge today to examine it for repairs, and I think we can wait another winter before we redo the floorboards."

The bridge didn't need repairs? That wasn't the reason behind this meeting.

"While I was checking out the floorboards, though, I discovered that someone is keeping hooch there, by the crate loads. It must be a whiskey runner's stash."

Winnie sucked in her breath, pulling the air away from everyone else in the room. When Mary Anne remembered to breathe again, she sensed the current of anger vibrating among the people seated at the table.

"Whiskey runners? Here, in Maple Notch? I'd heard the rumors, but I'd hoped they weren't true," Aunt Flo said.

"At best it's someone's private stash, with enough whiskey to keep an alcoholic in liquor for the better part of a year. But whiskey runners seems a lot more likely. They're using it for a transfer point."

"Do you have any idea who put it there?" Clarinda asked. "Anyone local?"

Wallace shrugged. "Someone would have to know about the bridge, of course, but it's one of the more convenient places on the road heading down the Canada corridor. They could have been hunting for a likely spot and happened upon our bridge."

Mary Anne's spirits tumbled. She poured a glass of water and sipped it.

The people pursuing her would run whiskey from Canada to the big cities on the east coast. Maybe that was why the man she recognized at the restaurant was here.

Possibility was not the same thing as proof. She didn't know the man's name, nor the gang he was involved with. She didn't really know anything.

"Mary Anne." Wallace's voice cut through the fog. "You look troubled."

She straightened her spine and lifted her head. "It is distressing."

"You do know we'll do whatever is necessary to protect you." Although he was addressing the entire family, she felt as though he was speaking to her alone. "I would die before I'd let any harm come to you."

Wallace couldn't have made his feelings any clearer, and tears formed in Mary Anne's eyes. If he knew the truth about her, he would never say something like that.

A light rap sounded on the door and Wallace stood. "That should be the constable, Gerard. I called him earlier."

Cops.

She couldn't mention her suspicions. Not when cops were involved.

Chapter 19

The weekend passed without any further incident. On Monday morning, Wallace hesitated at the second-floor landing, wondering if Mary Anne had awakened. With the excuse of asking her to fact-check the manuscript, he could explore her thoughts on his account of finding hooch under the bridge. Gauging by her reaction, he'd guess she knew something about it.

Connecting whiskey to Mary Anne didn't make sense. He hadn't seen her drink anything stronger than an egg cream. At least not the Mary Anne he knew today. Would he have said the same thing about the young woman who arrived in Maple Notch six months ago? He didn't know, and he didn't like the fact that he didn't know.

She had a right to leave her past behind, but in her letter, she mentioned bringing danger upon them. Had she brought it to Maple Notch?

He trotted down the stairs. After seeking God's will in

prayer, he wanted to speak with one of the wisest people he knew.

Clarinda wasn't in her usual spot in the kitchen. Sounds of retching from the back of the house reached Wallace. She was *never* sick to the stomach, except of course when...

He put the teakettle on to boil and fixed some cinnamon toast. When she joined him a few minutes later, he handed her tea and toast. "I've been told this is good for an upset stomach."

Clarinda's wan smile confirmed his suspicions.

"How far along...?"

"I'm not even sure yet. At least, I wasn't sure, until I got sick this morning."

As Clarinda munched through two slices of toast and two cups of tea, color returned to her face. "So, talk to me about Mary Anne."

Of course she had guessed the reason he sought her out. "I can't help thinking she knows more about the whiskey than she lets on."

"I agree." Clarinda looked thoughtful as she poured more tea for both of them. "Her letter mentioned a real threat. I assumed she meant her life was in danger, but perhaps she meant something more." She closed her mouth, as if unwilling to give voice to the unthinkable.

"Like being involved with whiskey runners in some way?" Wallace said. "I want to protect her, but I can't if I don't know what she's running from." He ran his hand through his hair and plunked his elbows on the table. "What should I do?"

Clarinda drew a deep breath. "The constable has the situation under control here. As far as Mary Anne goes...I'm sure you've been talking with the Lord about all this, as I have. What comes to my mind is His command, 'Judge not that ye be not judged.'"

Wallace wanted nothing more than to do just that, to ignore Mary Anne's possible association with the whiskey runners. "But she said—"

"She said she was in danger. We know very little about her life before she arrived in Maple Notch."

Make that so little that it wouldn't register on a postage scale. "You think she's not involved?"

"I think we don't know. She won't keep quiet if she thinks we're in danger. She promised us that, and I trust her. More importantly, do you?"

The question stopped Wallace. He wanted to trust Mary Anne. He did trust her, yet at the same time, he didn't. "Close your mouth before a fly camps out on your tongue." Clarinda buttered a slice of bread and took a bite. "What she needs more than anything else is time. Time to work everything through her mind and tell us what's troubling her. I have an idea of something that might help speed things up."

She reached in a drawer behind her and pulled out an envelope. "Howard surprised me with plans for a trip to New York to see the Ziegfield Follies for our tenth anniversary, but under the circumstances, I won't be making the trip." She slid the envelope across the table to Wallace. "Maybe a trip to New York with Winnie and Mary Anne will give you the answers you are looking for."

"Miss Laurents! You have company," Winnie's friend, Louise Sawtelle, said.

Mary Anne glanced up from the Bible she was devouring by reading large chunks every day. Reading the words in print made them real and alive in a new way. Placing a bookmark to note where she stopped, she opened the door. "I have company?"

"It's Mr. Tuttle. He brought Winnie back, and they're waiting to see you in the front parlor."

"I'll be right down."

With the dismissal, Louise vanished in the direction of her room. Mary Anne took a minute to examine her closet. She shouldn't care what she was wearing when she saw Wallace, but she did. If she wasn't at the school, she might dab on a bit of lipstick, but Aunt Flo disapproved of the practice.

The clock indicated she had spent five minutes worrying about her appearance. *Vain woman.* After pulling a spring green cardigan over her blouse, she walked down the stairs.

Three Tuttles—Aunt Flo had joined Wallace and Winnie—waited for Mary Anne. Upon Mary Anne's entry, Winnie broke into a wide smile.

Aunt Flo spoke first. "Wallace came to me with a most wonderful suggestion. He asked me to assure you that you have my permission for a few days' absence from work."

Absence from work? Mary Anne's mind whirled with possibilities.

"We're going to New York." The words burst forth from Winnie.

"Winnie!" Wallace's scolding held a bit of laughter. "You didn't give me a chance to ask her properly."

"New York?" Saying the words made Mary Anne weak, and she sank into the nearest chair.

"Howard was planning a trip to New York for their tenth anniversary, but then…" Wallace's face grew red.

"Clarinda discovered she is expecting and does not feel up to traveling." Aunt Flo didn't find the topic of her niece's "delicate condition" inappropriate for their conversation.

Wallace's face returned to its normal color now that Aunt Flo had delivered the embarrassing news. "He had purchased tickets to the Ziegfield Follies and doesn't want them to go to waste. Please say you'll go with us." He grinned as if he were Santa Claus opening his sack on Christmas Eve.

The Follies. She had never seen the show, although she had

heard wonderful things about it. But… "That's two tickets, and there are three of us."

"I already took care of that. I called them today and made a reservation for a third person, hoping you would say yes. I even requested the hotel change the room to a suite with two rooms." Pleading gray eyes widened behind his glasses. How could she say no? How could she say yes?

Mary Anne touched her hair, a habit she had developed lately in comparing her present circumstances with the past. "New York…." Her voice trailed off.

"Please say yes. Imagine. New York City. Skating in Central Park. Seeing a live show." With a glance at her brother's amused eye, Winnie added, "And the art museum and the Bronx Zoo. Oh, I'd love to see it all." Her dark eyes glittered.

"You can't see all that in a week," Wallace reminded her.

"But I can see a lot of it." Winnie spun around on the carpet, imitating one of the skating moves she had perfected.

It's not all that special. Not when you've lived there all your life. "It's only October. You can't go ice skating yet," Mary Anne said.

Wallace's widening smile told Mary Anne she had lost the argument. "So you'll come with us?"

"I don't have much choice." Flickers of warmth curled in her stomach, and she decided maybe, just maybe, it wouldn't be so bad.

A couple of nights later, she wasn't so sure. After spending three hours packing in Winnie's room, they still hadn't finished.

"I can't believe Aunt Flo let me take off from school. She said something about not all education taking place in the classroom." Winnie tucked her Bible and a single school book at the bottom of her suitcase. "Education, my foot. I intend to have fun."

"You'll have lessons to do while we're gone," Mary Anne

reminded her. "And if Aunt Flo's not satisfied with it, she'll give you more to do when you get back."

"Oh, I know." Winnie shook out a sweater she had packed, held it against her body and hung it back in the closet. "I can't decide what to wear. All I have that fits me right are school uniforms and the clothes I skate in. Nothing seems right for the city."

"Clarinda made you a new dress in only two days' time." Mary Anne pointed to the wine-colored frock. Its simple lines flattered Winnie's girlish figure and brought a shine to her cheeks.

"But that's only one dress, and we'll be there for days."

Mary Anne stifled her qualms that Winnie's worry raised. "Your skating clothes might be the perfect choice for a day at Central Park or at the zoo. You don't want to wear your best dress when you're walking between monkeys and lions."

Winnie rewarded Mary Anne with a giggle. "I suppose not."

"Add a sweater to your best summer dress, and it will be good for fall." Mary Anne repeated the same advice she had offered several times throughout the night. If Winnie remained like this all weekend, Mary Anne doubted either one would get any sleep. Was this what she missed by not having any brothers or sisters? Seeing the bright color blooming in the girl's cheeks, the joy beaming from her eyes, Mary Anne decided she had missed a lot. How much better would it be to have a daughter someday to share exciting events with?

She'd love it.

After the length of time it took Winnie and Mary Anne to pack for the trip, Wallace feared they would have two trunks and five hat boxes each. Their two valises came as a pleasant surprise. His extra suit, for the visit with his editor, and his manuscript, required a large carpetbag. "What are you thinking about?" Mary Anne's voice fell like morning dewdrops.

Frowning, he pointed at the floor where his carpetbag rested. "I'm not satisfied with what I've written. I'm afraid the editor will reject it." First he helped Winnie, then Mary Anne, into the Model T.

"You always said that before you handed in a term paper. And you always got As. You can write. Even Aunt Flo says so." Winnie nodded firmly.

Wallace hid a smile. As the resident academic, Aunt Flo was the expert on everything in Winnie's eyes. "There's a difference between writing for school and writing for people you want to buy your book. John James Audubon wasn't the first person fascinated with birds, but he interested other people as well."

"Audubon is your hero." Mary Anne tucked her traveling skirt, a sensible dark blue to hide any grime from the journey, around her legs. "But you shouldn't worry. I've seen some of his sketches. Yours are as good as his—even better, in fact."

"It doesn't matter. Ready or not, my editor wants the manuscript now." They had reached the old bridge, and Wallace stopped before crossing.

As they pulled into the darkness, Mary Anne's chuckle reached him. "I'll never forget to stop before entering a covered bridge again."

"I'm glad we had the accident. If not for that, we might never have met." Wallace pulled his lips together to keep from saying anything else so revealing.

Mary Anne flicked a surprised look in his direction before staring out the side window. "How far is it until we cross into the state of New York?" She craned her neck, looking at the canopy of leaves dancing against the sky. "There's a bald eagle overhead."

She must have driven this part of the road at night when

she came to Vermont. If so, she had missed the beautiful countryside except in brief snatches, by headlight. "It's close to a hundred miles from home. Three hundred miles to New York City."

A brief pang tapped his heart. If only they could take their time making this trip. After a glance at Mary Anne, he suspected she felt the same way. On the other hand, Winnie couldn't wait to arrive. If she could have climbed in an airplane and flown instead, she would have been happy.

When his parents were Wallace's age, they would have laughed at the idea of making a trip to New York in a single day. If the three of them made the trip in a brougham, they would have all the time they could want to enjoy the scenery. Now the world hurled forward in a rush.

But he could, and would, make a short stop for lunch, at the south end of Lake Champlain. He wouldn't let Mary Anne leave Vermont without seeing the body of water that played a central part in its history.

He turned onto the road leading to Fort Ticonderoga, at the narrows feeding into the south end of the lake. His family had a strong connection to the Fort, one Winnie could tell as well as he could. He couldn't think of a better place to revisit their past.

Chapter 20

Mary Anne sat at the picnic table outside the ruined fort and wished time could stand still so she could remain here forever.

In such a peaceful spot, with water and trees surrounding them, she was able to see a long distance in all directions. It was hard to imagine that two battles took place at the fort during the Revolutionary War. A sign explained that during the first battle, the Americans won Ticonderoga from the British, but the British won it back during the second.

Back against the table and facing the opposite direction, Wallace sat beside her. Winnie wandered among the ruins. The Tuttle family's roots went back before the Revolutionary War, all in the same place. Imagine that. That kind of stability must give the Tuttles a sense of identity she'd never had.

The rainclouds which had spilled moisture on Vermont all month had taken a break, allowing her to see the surrounding countryside. Houses and communities dotted the once virgin forest. Even now, this mountaintop was a world removed from the city of her childhood. Which America had her grandparents come in search of—the supposed "streets paved with gold" in New York, or the undeveloped land she had seen today? Her family had added its own flavor to the country's melting pot. They had left behind everything known for something better.

Winnie wandered back, a handful of wet leaves and rocks in her hands.

"You're not bringing those in the car," Wallace said.

Frowning, Winnie dropped them on the ground. Mary Anne bent over and picked up one of the leaves, the gorgeous pointed shape of the maple leaf, in a rich orange-red.

Wallace picked up one as well. "They say each one is different. Each bird is different. Each person." He brought his leaf next to hers and examined them side by side. "Both are obviously maple leaves. But the veins in this one are a little different from yours."

His head was so close to hers, his lips so tantalizingly close. She ran her tongue over her lower lip and wondered if he wanted to kiss her. His eyes skittered in Mary Anne's direction, and she knew he did. Moments like this, she could forget her past. Her future was what mattered—a future with him. Safe. Protected. Cherished. Able to move ahead with all that God had in store for her. The longing she thought she saw in his eyes reflected what was in her heart.

Winnie scuffed the leaves with the toe of her shoe. "We need to leave if we want to get to New York tonight."

How Mary Anne wished they could linger, to walk the grounds of the fort, to paddle a canoe on the lake. Imagine the birds they would see. But if they didn't get to New York tonight, they might miss the show tomorrow.

Another time. Wallace mouthed the words where only Mary Anne could see, and pink flashed in his cheeks. To distract attention from his discomfort, she broke the leftover bread into three pieces, one for each of them. The three of them tore it into small pieces, and blue jays swooped down to enjoy the feast. Stuffing the remaining trash in a paper sack, Wallace led them back to the Model T. Next stop, New York City.

Darkness had fallen by the time they reached the outskirts of New York. Lights illuminated the urban landscape, throwing the view into an eternal gray, revealing and hiding at the same time. Their Model T squeezed through the narrow streets.

"Is this where you lived, Mary Anne?" If it was daytime, Winnie would have stuck her head out the window. So far the sights consisted of homes, stores and not much else.

"No." Mary Anne didn't elaborate. The last thing she needed on this trip was a visit to her old home in Brooklyn, where she would run into dozens of people ready to report Marabelle's reappearance in the neighborhood. Better to stay in Manhattan, where Wallace wouldn't go anywhere near a speakeasy. "People think of New York as one city, but it's really five boroughs. There's the Bronx, Queens, Brooklyn and Staten Island. And Manhattan, of course, where we're headed."

"The island the Lenape Indians sold to the Dutch for about a thousand dollars." Winnie grinned. "We're studying American history this fall. But we have to go the Bronx to see the zoo, don't we?"

Wallace nodded. "If we have time."

"And we want to meet your family, too, Mary Anne." Winnie patted Mary Anne's hand.

Wallace drew in his breath but Mary Anne didn't blame the girl. She had given voice to the question that was uppermost in Wallace's mind.

"I did think you would want to visit your father's grave."

Wallace looked at her quickly, then returned his attention to the street. At the next intersection, he turned right.

Daddy. Mary Anne's mouth went dry. She didn't even know where he was buried. In her hurry to leave the city, she had asked her pastor to make arrangements in her place. But Wallace offered the opportunity to visit his burial plot, to cry for all that had been and was no more. Her throat clogged.

"Something to think about." Wallace turned onto another street.

She nodded, grateful that he didn't press for an answer. As he made more turns, she recognized landmarks. He was heading for the heart of the city. "Where are we staying?"

"The Waldorf-Astoria." He said it matter-of-factly, as if everyone who visited New York stayed at the premier hotel.

"That's pretty fancy."

Wallace shrugged. "Howard already made the reservations, and he figured we might as well take advantage of it."

Unfortunately, the Waldorf-Astoria was the sort of place her former associates frequented.

Wallace fingered the tweed of his suit coat, bought for his graduation from college. Recent years had seen some strange fads, like the raccoon coats popularized by the Four Horsemen of Notre Dame. Leather jackets—like the one worn by Charles Lindbergh when he crossed the Atlantic back in May—had even made an appearance in Maple Notch.

Wallace had ignored those styles, but he did like how he looked in a well-fitting suit, even if the new style made his shoulders look as thin as a boy's.

What would the girls wear tonight? A whistle escaped through his lips, and he moved in front of the mirror to straighten his tie. Tonight they would enjoy the Ziegfield Follies at the New Amsterdam Theatre. He couldn't tell which prospect excited Winnie more: dressing up, seeing the show or staying up long past her normal bedtime.

Plans for tomorrow were undecided. Winnie might sleep half the day away, or she might bounce out of bed at dawn, ready for more New York adventures.

The grandfather clock pinged, and he rapped on the door between their rooms. Winnie swung the door open, with a smiling Mary Anne behind her. Mary Anne wore a bright blue silk dress with hints of pink, her hair styled with more curls than usual, her tiny feet balanced on high heels. But she was pushing Winnie forward, expecting Wallace to praise his sister's appearance.

"What have you done with my sister?" Wallace pretended to look behind her. "This can't be Winnifred Tuttle."

Winnie giggled, and he relaxed. She wore a simple blue skirt with a sailor's shirt with red braid, patriotic colors always in style. Her hair was brushed back, rolled around her face but falling in a gentle twist down her back. Due to her excitement, she needed no artificial color on her cheeks. Black, low-heeled pumps graced her feet.

Wallace wanted to hug his sister like the little girl she always would be in his eyes, but he settled for blowing a kiss in her direction. "I will be the envy of every gentleman at the show tonight, with two such fine ladies on my arms."

With that, he slipped his arms underneath Mary Anne's right elbow and Winnie's left and headed out the door. Thanks to his calling ahead, a Checker cab was waiting for them at the front door.

The New Amsterdam Theatre was a short ride from the hotel. They walked through the painted arch, and he stared in amazement at the intricate friezes on the walls.

"How will we ever find our seats?" Winnie's eyes swept from side to side of the large building.

Wallace had never been in a theater this big before, but he knew how seating worked. "Let's get our coats checked first."

In this sparkling environment, Wallace could pretend he and Mary Anne were an ordinary couple enjoying a special night together. If this was their Cinderella moment, he prayed midnight would never arrive.

After pocketing the coat check stubs, he approached an usher and showed him their tickets.

"Come this way, please." The usher led them quickly to their seats, about halfway up the center section. No need for opera glasses from this spot.

Wallace sat between the girls. What would Mary Anne think if he gave in to his wish to slip his arm around her shoulders? No, if he did that, she might think he wanted to take advantage of her.

Seeking to keep his mind off the woman next to him, he studied the program. Soon he was caught up in the history of the theater. Built around 1902 in the art nouveau style, it was the largest theater in New York. The orchestra began the opening number, and he put the program aside.

The evening sped by. Eddie Cantor headlined a group of performers which also included Cliff Edwards and Claire Luce. The Ziegfeld Girls came and left the stage so quickly Wallace didn't know how they found time to change their elaborate costumes between sets.

As much fun as Wallace had watching the stage, watching Mary Anne was even better. He had feared she might find the performance boring, something she had seen several times. She had seen *The Mikado* on Broadway, after all. But although she controlled her reactions better than Winnie—all enthusiasm, laughter and applause—the same delight shone from her eyes.

They laughed, they cried, they cheered until their voices were hoarse and clapped until their hands turned red. Howard had made a good plan, wanting to bring Clarinda to New York for an unforgettable holiday. Wallace hoped to make i up to them in the future.

At long last the magical evening ended. Wallace had no idea how they were going to find a cab in the crowd of seventeen hundred people all trying to exit the theater at once He found an empty spot on a bench near the coat check.

"Let's wait here." Winnie plopped down, fatigue showing in her face while her eyes glazed over.

Mary Anne stayed on her feet, seemingly no more eager than Wallace for the evening to end. "Oh, that was wonderful. Thank you so much for bringing me."

Knots of people made their way out the theater doors. Beside Wallace, Mary Anne tensed before slipping into the space between him and the wall.

Following the direction of her gaze, he spotted two flappers, one with raven hair and one with blond. He much preferred Mary Anne's brand of beauty.

The raven-haired woman looked their way and raised a hand in greeting. "If it isn't Marabelle Lamont, returned from the dead."

Chapter 21

Mary Anne knew Wallace had heard Eva's greeting. His entire body stiffened, making his lovely suit sit on his shoulders awkwardly.

He relaxed so quickly that she had to be paying close attention to notice his reaction. The way Winnie was studying the friezes on the wall, she might not have noticed a fire engine if it plowed into the room.

Wallace shifted position, so that Mary Anne was largely hidden from sight. "If you don't react, she might decide she made a mistake. Unless you want to speak to her?"

Mary Anne shook her head, but her heart pounded. Eva wasn't a bad sort, one of the first to accept "Marabelle" into her group. That was the problem. A woman who rarely met a person she didn't like, Eva would report the reappearance of Marabelle to any who would stand still long enough to listen.

Wallace kept a smile on his face. "The crowd has thinned enough for us to leave by the side exit. Tie your scarf over your hair and I'll help you into your coat. We can make a quiet departure."

He touched Winnie as if to ask if she was ready to go. She jumped to her feet, and Mary Anne was blocked from view on two sides. The crack of light visible between Wallace's side and the wall revealed that Eva was still in the lobby. Confusion reigned on her face as she swiveled around.

Mary Anne didn't stand yet. With her high heels, she was several inches taller than Winnie, and she made a snap decision and slipped the shoes off. The theater had seen worse things than shoeless feet. Wallace raised his eyebrows but tucked the shoes into the enormous pockets on the inside of his coat.

"What are you—" Winnie asked.

Wallace brought his finger to his lips. "We're making a quiet exit. I'll explain later." He waited until a large group pushed through the theater doors, hiding them from Eva's view. He nodded and Mary Anne headed for the door. Winnie trotted behind them quietly.

They found themselves at the corner of 8th Avenue and 42nd Street, in the heart of the city's theater district. If they dared go to Broadway, they'd find their pick of cabs. But that was the most likely direction that Eva would take.

"There's a cab." Relief flooded Wallace's voice. "Let's get back to the hotel."

"Do we have to?" Winnie held back. "I spotted a coffee shop across the street."

"Perhaps another night. I'll explain later." Wallace followed the women into the waiting cab. "The Waldorf-Astoria, please."

Winnie chattered about the marvelous, amazing, unforgettable show all the way back to the hotel. Mary Anne didn't interrupt her, her pensive expression suggesting she was deeply troubled.

When they entered the hotel, Wallace stopped by the front desk. He returned a few minutes later, rubbing his hands together. "That settles it. The Waldorf-Astoria has started something new, called room service. I've asked them to deliver a coffee and dessert tray to our suite."

Back in their rooms, Winnie squealed with delight when she saw the square of chocolate laid on her pillow case and the thick pink robe laid across the quilt. "Since we're not going out, I think I'll take a long bubble bath and put on this warm robe."

"An excellent idea." Wallace waited until she disappeared into the bath before he turned to Mary Anne. "Perhaps we can have a moment of private conversation out on the balcony?"

Mary Anne slipped a shawl over her shoulders and followed him out the doors. The city of New York, her home for most of her life, spread out before them. She loved and feared it in equal measure. Wallace joined her at the railing, seemingly as entranced with the view as she was.

"Who was she?" Wallace asked.

The serenity of the panorama vanished. "Someone I used to know." Mary Anne shrugged.

Wallace drew in a deep breath. He must have a thousand questions. It would almost be easier if he demanded answers. Instead, he turned his back to the city view and placed his hand over hers. "Tomorrow is a free day. It might be a good time to visit your father's grave."

Wallace gently squeezed Mary Anne's fingers, before holding them in a loose grip. She welcomed their soft touch, his implied support.

Daddy. Even a visit to her pastor, to learn where her father was buried, involved risk. But she owed that much to her father—she owed it to herself—to see his grave and say a final goodbye.

"That's a good idea."

Wallace lifted her hand to his lips and kissed her fingers.

"But there's something I have to do first." The whole truth teetered on the tip of Mary Anne's tongue, but she struggled to find the words to explain. Someone rapped on the door, carrying the room service tray, and the opportunity was lost.

They ate everything on the dessert tray, so much food that Mary Anne's dress size would surely increase if they ate so many sweets every night during their stay.

"Tomorrow I want to go to Central Park." Winnie wanted to pack as much as possible into every day of their trip.

Mary Anne looked at Wallace, waiting for him to offer an explanation. He said, "Mary Anne has something else in mind. Tell us about it."

His gray eyes gently twinkled. He was forcing her into an explanation, even more, into a commitment.

"I want to visit my father's grave. But the truth is I'm not sure where he's buried."

Wallace settled his back against his chair when she said that.

"I had to leave home in a hurry. I asked our pastor to take care of Daddy's burial. So before we go to his grave, I need to speak with the pastor." Even as she said the words, Mary Anne knew she wanted to see the man who had counseled her, prayed for her and led her to the Lord. "There's a phone in the parsonage, so we can call and set up an appointment to see him."

The safest plan might be to ask her question over the phone. But Mary Anne was tired of playing it safe. The time had come for her to reassure her spiritual mentor that his prayers had been answered. She had returned to the Lord, and God had placed a godly man in her path.

She didn't say any more. Wallace brought his hands together. "So that's what we'll do tomorrow. And on the way

Mary Anne can point out birds that live here in New York that we don't have in Vermont."

"Birds." Winnie huffed, but at least Wallace's comment had taken her mind off her disappointment. "I'm sorry about your father, though. I know what it's like to lose your parents."

Mama and Daddy. Lord willing, tomorrow Mary Anne would enjoy a return to her roots and not worry about the mess she had made for herself.

Wallace took in the rows of houses that lined the streets as the cab drove into Brooklyn. They probably were nice enough inside, but he couldn't imagine growing up so close to his neighbors. If these people opened their windows during the summer, they'd smell the bacon cooking next door, hear crying infants.

"We're close." Mary Anne leaned forward in the backseat, more excited than he'd ever seen her. "There's the church." She announced it in such a way that he might have expected the splendor of the New Amsterdam or perhaps Saint Patrick's Cathedral.

Instead it was a brick church, in a traditional style, with a steeple at the front and a sloping slate roof. A small plate at the front announced it as Good Shepherd Church, Pastor: Charles Asher.

"The parsonage is right next door." Mary Anne climbed out of the car as soon as the driver parked.

Wallace didn't know what to expect of the people who had known Mary Anne in her previous life. Was Mrs. Asher interested in fashion, wearing the modern clothing favored by young women nowadays? Or was she more like Aunt Flo, given to a timeless fashion that stamped dignity on its wearer?

A pleasant, round-faced woman with puffs of gray-blond

hair framing her face opened the door as soon as they stepped on the porch. "Mary Anne Lamont, as I live and breathe!"

That answered one question. Mary Anne Lamont was her real name, as she had confessed.

"Mrs. Asher!" Mary Anne threw herself into the older woman's arms but quickly withdrew. "I'll finish introductions as soon as we get inside."

Mrs. Asher led them into a cozy sitting room that looked like a page out of an old issue of *Godey's Lady's Book*. The furniture looked as if it had withstood more than one generation of children—good, solid pieces that suggested permanence. "My husband will be home soon. One of our parishioners—Mr. Garrett, Mary Anne, you remember him, I'm sure—passed away last night."

Nodding, Mary Anne took her seat. "Mrs. Asher, I'd like you to meet my friends, Wallace and Winnie Tuttle. Their family has been kind enough to give me a home the last few months."

"Mr. Tuttle, Miss Tuttle, glad to meet you. Thank you for taking care of our treasure here." Mrs. Asher patted Mary Anne on the shoulder. "Would you care for some refreshments? I have some fruit ready."

Mary Anne shook her head—she hadn't wanted much breakfast either—but Winnie nodded. Their hostess disappeared in the direction of the kitchen.

A few books lay on top of the lamp table, and Mary Anne picked them up. She read the first book's title with pride. "*Pilgrim's Progress.* He's not talking about the Pilgrims who landed at Plymouth Rock, is he?"

"No. It's a classic allegory of the Christian life," Wallace said. "You might enjoy reading it. I'm sure Aunt Flo has a copy."

Mrs. Asher returned to the sitting room as he said that. Her eyes widened as she saw the book in Mary Anne's hands.

"You're looking at a book." The way she said it betrayed her knowledge of Mary Anne's secret.

"Yes." Mary Anne's answer held laughter. "A lot has changed since I left."

A smile hinted at Mrs. Asher's mouth. "Well, if you want to read it you can take that with you when you leave."

"Thank you. I'd like that." Mary Anne handled the book like a prize at the county fair before tucking it into her purse.

"Mary Anne, look at you." A warm, gruff voice called from the back room, and the man who must be the pastor folded her in a crushing hug.

Wallace contented himself with listening to the flow of conversation. Winnie told of Mary Anne's wins in the scripture memory and reading competition, and Mrs. Asher clapped in delight. After they finished the fruit, Mrs. Asher brought out sandwiches and cookies. Mary Anne's appetite returned, and she helped demolish the food.

"I am so glad to see you so well settled." Pastor Asher clasped Mary Anne's hands in his. "You mentioned your father's grave when you called. Your father had purchased a double plot when your mother passed, and so they are buried together. Do you know the cemetery?"

Mary Anne nodded. "Thank you so much. And now, we really shouldn't keep you any longer. I'll help clean up, and we'll be on our way."

Pastor Asher took Wallace aside while the ladies disappeared into the kitchen. He looked the way Wallace's father had reacted when Howard first came calling on Clarinda. "I've known Mary Anne all her life."

Wallace had noticed that the Ashers called her Mary Anne, not Marabelle. Maybe her fancy name was a passing phase.

"Since her father has gone home to be with the Lord, I feel it's my duty to inquire. How are things between the two of you? I can't say how relieved I am to discover the Lord brought her to your home, but what about the future?"

Here, in this place, with a man who cared so much about Mary Anne, Wallace could speak the truth. "I'd give my life to protect her. I'd like to marry her, if she'll have me."

The pastor smiled. "I am glad to hear it, although we will be sorry to lose her. My prayers go with you for your safety. She never told me exactly what happened, but as far as I know, her father's murderer was never caught."

Chapter 22

In preparation for going to the cemetery, Mary Anne wore the darkest skirt she had brought with her and the dullest blouse, covered with a black cardigan. She'd even found a black scarf to drape across her head. The autumn sunshine mocked her mood as they approached the graveyard, a wrought iron gate all that stood between her and her parents' graves. Not much had changed since Daddy brought her to visit on Decoration Day last year.

Wallace and Winnie walked on either side of her. She caught Wallace looking at her a few times, and she wondered if Pastor Asher had said something to arouse his curiosity further.

The graves lay straight ahead ten rows, and five to the right. This was her past; and God willing, Winnie and Wallace represented her future. Mary Anne wanted to be alone when she said goodbye. "I'll go on by myself, if you don't mind."

Without waiting for an answer, she lifted the latch on the gate and entered. Someone maintained the area with care. In spite of the leaves dropping from the trees with every brush of wind, the grounds were immaculate. Oak and elm trees had lost half of their leaves, somewhat like her feelings on this day, half lost, half hopeful.

Five plots in, she came upon her father's gravestone: Jack Raymond Lamont. *Oh, Daddy.* For the first time, she could read the words on her mother's grave marker: Anna Maria Lamont. *Mama, I hope you're proud of me.* She sat on the ground between the graves, heedless of the tears.

She heard feet rustling through the grass but ignored them. Let each person mourn in peace. "Mama, Daddy, it's been hard, but I'm going to be okay. I might not get to come back again, but don't worry about me. I've met a good man. Maybe *the* man."

"Well, that's good to hear, Marabelle. Or should I call you Mary Anne Laurents?"

That voice. Mary Anne's back stiffened. Pretending a case of mistaken identity wouldn't work this time, with her sitting in front of her parents' graves, evidence of fresh tears on her face.

Wallace. She had to find him. She grabbed her purse, jumped to her feet, and starting running. But Wallace had disappeared with Winnie.

The man—she had never learned his name—caught her within two strides. "You aren't getting away this time. We have some business to settle."

All of her strength was as helpless against her captor as someone trying to break concrete by throwing pebbles at it. Yanking her arms, he dragged her across the grass while her shoes dug into the sod. The man shoved her into a waiting car.

"Wallace!" She flung his name into the wind.

The man climbed in after her, a gun pointed at her head.

"Say another word, lady, and you'll end up like your father."
He pulled a burlap sack over her head.

Oh, God, help me now.

After Mary Anne left them at the gate, Wallace and Winnie stared at each other. "What can we do while we wait?"
Winnie was as restless as a first-grader at recess, a bundle of energy ready to explode across the schoolyard.

Wallace didn't want to stray far from Mary Anne. They could wander among the gravestones, as long as they left Mary Anne alone. "What do you think about visiting the cemetery?"

Winnie laughed. "Did Aunt Flo suggest that? She said I could learn about the people who made up New York by visiting a cemetery. Things like names and dates and even the language on the gravestones. But I don't have a notebook."

"It's a good thing I'm prepared." Wallace pulled his sketchbook from his pocket. If he could find a quiet spot, he'd sketch Mary Anne's picture. But she wouldn't want her grief captured on paper. Who would?

Winnie grabbed the sketchbook and pencil and capered down the path to the left, away from Mary Anne. "It looks like there are older markers over this way."

That was as good a reason as any to see that section. Wallace put his hands in his pockets and followed at a slower pace. Names here ranged from familiar British names to more foreign surnames: Novak, Ivanov, Salo. Ivanov sounded Russian, but he didn't have a clue about the other names.

Winnie sat on a bench within sight of three or four graves, scribbling down information. In this peaceful place, people could visit their loved ones and perhaps consider their own mortality. How he wanted to offer Mary Anne comfort, but she had asked him to stay away.

"Wallace!"

He sprang to his feet and hurtled in the direction of her cry. On the street, a man in a black coat pushed her into a waiting car.

The car pulled away from the curb before he made it halfway down the lane. He reached the street in time to see the car, an ordinary Model T, turn at the corner.

Her father's murderer was never caught.

Wallace had promised to protect Mary Anne, but he had failed at the first test. *God, help her.*

The burlap sack disoriented Mary Anne and the close smell of dust and grain made her stomach roll as she bounced up and down on the seat.

"I can't believe you came back to New York. Teasing fate isn't a good idea." Smoke mixed with the air seeping through the burlap. "When the picture of Mary Anne Laurents showed up in that Vermont newspaper, I decided she couldn't be you. I didn't know whether to believe Eva when she said her good friend Marabelle Lamont had returned. Imagine my surprise when I discovered she was staying at the Waldorf-Astoria. You had left the hotel by the time I got the news, so I decided to keep my eye on your father's grave."

Mary Anne didn't want to give the man the satisfaction of fainting. Instead, she breathed slowly and carefully as she pieced together what she had learned. Eva did know the man who had killed her father, probably through the social circles where bathtub gin was the beverage of choice.

The car stopped, and once again cold steel pressed against Mary Anne's neck. "You're going to have a little talk with my boss. You tell him what he wants, if you know what's good for you."

He prodded her forward, and she stumbled out of the car and up a couple of steps, into a room filled with smoke and the stench of sour liquor. The man pushed her into a chair and tied her hands behind her back. Nearby, someone scratched a match, and she smelled sulfur and fresh cigar smoke.

"Miss Lamont. I have been waiting to meet you a long time." A chair squeaked, and heavy steps crossed the room, stopping in front of her. "Rocco, leave us alone."

Rocco. First name or last name?

The door opened and closed. The faceless voice spoke to her again. "You and your father led us on a merry chase, Miss Lamont. Your father took something that didn't belong to him. You don't steal from me and get away with it."

Daddy hadn't stolen the money. He won it in a lottery, but he wasn't supposed to win. Rage and paralyzing fear stormed through Mary Anne's veins. Rocco had shot her father as he sat in the same position Mary Anne was in now.

How cruel it would be to die this way, here and now. She'd never even told Wallace that she cared for him.

The account of Saint Stephen's martyrdom ran through her mind. She didn't have his faith or stoicism in facing her own imminent death.

"After all the trouble you've caused us, I should just shoot you now. But I don't like losing money. Maybe you can still be of use to us. Now, this is what I want you to do…."

Wallace headed to the Waldorf-Astoria, kicking a few lampposts along the way. He felt like cursing, but he hadn't done that since Mom had washed his mouth out with soap and Dad had reminded him why Christians didn't cuss.

He was so angry, felt such a sense of futility, of helplessness. After he had left Winnie at the hotel, with strict orders not to open the door to anyone, he'd headed for the nearest police station. They didn't understand the urgency of the situation, even when he offered the hypothesis that the man who had kidnapped Mary Anne might have been behind her father's death.

No, they questioned him as if he were a suspect. What was her father's name? Lamont, he didn't know his first name. When did he die? Sometime before the first of April.

The officer scratched his head and said he couldn't help without more specific information. Taking Wallace's contact information, the officer promised to get in touch if he learned anything.

When traffic at the next intersection halted his progress, Wallace realized his folly. With the police refusing to help, he had cursed the only One who could protect Mary Anne. He glanced at the sky, what little of it could be seen above the skyscrapers. *Forgive me, Lord, and don't take out my sin on Mary Anne.*

At the hotel, he raced up the steps two at a time and knocked on their door. "It's me, Wallace."

A white-faced Winnie opened the door for him. "What did the police say?"

"They can't help." Wallace closed his mouth, not wanting to let Winnie see the depth of his fear. "But the Ashers might know something. We'll go there next, and I'll ask them if you can stay with them."

She opened her mouth, but Wallace didn't let her speak. "I don't want you staying here on your own. How long will it take you to pack? In case you need to stay overnight?"

Wallace left the door between their rooms open while he decided if he should pack a few things himself. He couldn't think of anything, least of all his book manuscript. Its importance had vanished with Mary Anne. He poked his head back into the girls' room. "Pack a few of Mary Anne's things as well, please."

A man of God might kneel on the floor, but Wallace couldn't stay still. Prayers mixed with frantic thoughts as he paced back and forth.

"I'm ready," Winnie called, and he entered their room.

A key rattled in the lock, and Wallace jumped. *Settle down. It's just the hotel staff.*

A muddy shoe appeared in the doorway. "Winnie? Wallace?"

"Mary Anne!" Wallace opened the door as she collapsed in his arms. He held her close. "Thank God. I saw the man kidnap you. What happened?"

"He let me go."

A lot more was involved in her reappearance, he was sure, but it could wait. "Let me call room service and get you something to eat."

Winnie put an arm around Mary Anne when Wallace let her go. "Did that dreadful man hurt you?"

Mary Anne shook her head, but she jumped when a knock came at the door. "Who is it?" Wallace asked through the door.

"The police," came the muffled reply.

Mary Anne's face paled, and the hand holding her purse trembled. "The police?"

Everything about Mary Anne screamed her reluctance to talk with the police. But he wouldn't let her get away with it. Not this time.

Chapter 23

Dryness glued Mary Anne's tongue to the roof of her mouth and she couldn't speak.

"Well, are you Mary Anne Lamont, aka Marabelle Lamont, the daughter of Jack R. Lamont, or not?"

She nodded in reply. The police officer, Detective Olney, had allowed Wallace to remain during the interview at the police station. She wasn't sure how she felt about that. He would hear the entire, ugly truth. She wouldn't blame him if he disappeared from her life once he knew everything.

"We've been wanting to speak with you for quite a while, Miss Lamont. Reverend Asher told us you had gone out of town to visit family, but you never got in touch." Olney's frown didn't help.

"I did leave suddenly. Don't blame Pastor Asher; he didn't know exactly where I had gone. I just returned to town this week." Why hadn't he mentioned the police during their visit this morning?

"What were you doing on the morning of March 30, of this year? It was a Wednesday."

Mary Anne would never forget, but she couldn't force the words out. The detective gestured for his sergeant to bring her a glass of water. She drank half the glass in a single gulp and then sipped the rest. After she emptied the glass, she ran her tongue around her mouth, testing it for dryness. *Help me, Lord.* "I will tell you my story. But please let me tell it my way. Then you can ask me your questions."

Olney glanced at the clock and called for a stenographer. A petite blonde came in, her steno pad resting on her lap, a pen poised over the page.

Olney placed his hands on the table, ready to listen. "Go ahead."

Wallace's silent presence demanded, *Look at me while you tell your story. I will listen without judging.*

Mary Anne drew a deep breath and began. "It all started after Christmas. Daddy bought a lottery ticket from the local grocery store. He always did that, buying raffle tickets, never betting on games or horses, though. The most we ever won was two tickets to a Dodgers game." Her eyes misted at the memory.

"The St. Ignatius Children's Fund sponsored the lottery. And he won! Enough money to make us rich no matter how much we spent. He let me buy whatever I wanted. That's where the Marabelle business came from. I thought I was too good for plain old Mary Anne anymore. It didn't take me long to decide I didn't really like speakeasies and all that."

Wallace smiled, showing his acceptance of her story. So far.

"Does this have anything to do with your father's death?"

The detective was being oh-so-patient. Mary Anne didn't know if he was being nice, or giving her a chance to get caught in her own web.

"It does. Daddy told me I had to stop spending money so wildly. That made me mad, but I didn't know he'd had some visitors. The man at the grocery shop who ran the lottery begged him to return the prize money. He said the Children's Fund was a fraud, and Daddy had to give the money back to the sponsors."

The detective leaned in close. "What grocer was it?" Mary Anne gave him the details.

"But Daddy refused. I had already spent a lot of it, of course." Heat rushed into her cheeks. "But he thought the grocer was lying. He won the money fair and square, but he was willing to make arrangements with the Children's Fund if the grocer would just tell him who to talk to." Her fingers tapped nervously in her lap. "Can I have another glass of water?"

It came, and she drank it. Now for the last, hardest bit. "About a week passed. I had spent the night—Tuesday night, the twenty-ninth—with a friend. When I came home, a car I didn't recognize sat in front of our house. I parked around the corner and walked through our neighbor's backyard to our back door. When I opened the door, I saw him. Daddy."

Her voice cracked, and she waited until she could continue. "He was tied to a chair. A man wearing a black coat and gloves held a revolver in his hand. He demanded that Daddy give him back the money."

The detective jotted something down. "Would you recognize the man if you saw him again?" The detective drilled her to the back of her seat with his eyes.

"Yes." Mary Anne swallowed. "He's the same man who found me at the cemetery this morning."

Wallace leaned forward.

"Do you know his name? Or the name of the man he answers to?"

"They called him Rocco. I don't know any other names."

"I drew a picture of the man who kidnapped her, if that

will help." Wallace pulled his sketchbook out of his coat pocket and leafed through the pages.

"Rocco Fiori." The detective nodded in recognition and sent his sergeant on an errand. They waited until he returned.

The sergeant slid a photograph facedown across the table. Olney glanced at it and handed it to Mary Anne. "Is this the man Rocco took you to see this morning?"

Mary Anne didn't have to answer. The tremor in her arms and legs gave her away.

Detective Olney nodded as if satisfied. "I thought so. So the DiNapoli gang was behind the lottery. There were rumors back in March that they had suffered a major setback." A smile flickered across his face. "An ordinary man and a young woman dealt a blow to the DiNapoli gang."

Mary Anne failed to see humor in a situation that led to her father's death. "That's not all. I would gladly give him the money. It already cost me too much. But most of it is gone. He said not to worry, he had a job for me to do."

She looked at Wallace, begging him to understand. "He knows where I've been the past six months. And he wants my help in running whiskey from Canada down to New York City."

"I have to come with you. They're expecting to see me." Mary Anne crossed her arms over her chest, refusing the chair Wallace had pulled out for her.

Jacques Gerard, the town constable, had been brought up to speed as soon as they returned to Maple Notch. "This is no place for a woman." He spoke as if that settled it.

Wallace could have told him differently. In spite of the differences in their life stories, Mary Anne shared a certain boundless determination with his grandmother. They both would reject any reason other than sound logic.

Wallace couldn't think of one, but he had promised to protect her. How could he do that if she refused to stay where it was safe?

"I ran away when my father needed me. I won't do it again."

That kind of experience could change a person. The Wallace who emerged after his parents' deaths wasn't the same boy he had been before.

"She's right, you know." FBI agent John Smith—at least that was the name he gave them upon his arrival—spoke from his corner of the living room.

Triumph blossomed on Mary Anne's face and she sat, no longer afraid she'd be ousted from the discussion.

Smith spoke with implacable logic. "DiNapoli's men aren't stupid. They'll smell a setup a mile away. She has to meet them, alone, at the bridge, as she promised." He pointed at Mary Anne. "We want you to see if you can get them to agree to the place and time you suggest."

Mary Anne shook her head. "They already know I can't slip away before nightfall without someone noticing, so the time isn't a problem. But I can't tell them to meet me at the bridge without revealing I know their secret."

Was the woman determined to put herself in harm's way? Once she climbed into the car, she might never return.

Smith nodded. "One of my men will follow you, in case they change their minds. If they bring you to the bridge the way we expect them to, it's up to you to get them in sight of the cave. Have you been there before?"

Her dark eyes connected with Wallace's. "Not yet, but he's told me about it."

He had told her the family story of how his ancestors had taken refuge in the cave during the Revolutionary War. How strange that the same cave would play a part in his history as well. "We'll go tomorrow night, about the same time she expects to meet Rocco the next day, so she'll know what to expect."

Her smile reassured Wallace that things were all right between the two of them.

They stayed up late into the night, making plans. Smith's men would stay at the farm, minimizing comment in town.

The rest of the week sped by. Wallace waded through the editor's comments on his book. How unimportant the visit with his editor seemed now, compared to everything else that had happened during their trip to New York. Worrying about Mary Anne's future pushed the often cutting editorial remarks into insignificance. He took Mary Anne to the cave at sundown the night before Halloween. Aside from seeing her at church on Sunday, they had no other contact, and that was the hardest of all to bear. Never had he taken the Lord's command to pray without ceasing so seriously.

Constable Gerard had come out to the farmhouse the previous evening. "They'll be here tomorrow night." When the authorities made final arrangements, Smith almost demanded that Wallace stay home. He wasn't an officer of the law and had no authority. Neither Wallace nor Howard agreed.

On the night they expected the DiNapoli gang, they met with the federal agents and Constable Gerard in the cave by the bridge. God must have blinded the gangsters to it. A steady rain fell, gray clouds limiting visibility to a few feet in any direction.

"How will we be able to see Mary Anne in this mess?" Wallace fidgeted near the entrance, unable to pace out his anxiety in the cramped space. Rain sent cascading streams into the depths of the cave. The Feds sat as still as statues, as if they could wait until the next new moon without budging a muscle.

For supper, they ate cold sandwiches and drank coffee from a thermos, with men taking turns guarding the entrance. As the rain increased in intensity, water collected on the floor of the cave.

Wallace stepped to the entrance. Where once he could see riverbanks, a thin layer of water spilled. It licked at the edge of the cave and spilled into the interior, covering the soles of their shoes.

"They're here." Smith's voice whispered across the cave, and the men fell into position, poised to explode from the opening as soon as Mary Anne gave the signal.

The trickling water turned into a stream, rising past their ankles then their calves. *The bridge.* Wallace pushed past the entrance, heedless of discovery or flood.

"Mary Anne!"

With a groan deep enough to tear heaven in half, the bridge cracked and broke.

Chapter 24

Mary Anne saw the cresting river precious moments before DiNapoli's men did. She ran from beneath the bridge to the bank, where she gained a handhold.

The water tugged at her feet as she climbed into the limbs of the nearest tree. She wrapped arms and legs around the tree which had endured centuries of cold and ice, wind and rain. If anything survived this flood, the tree would.

"'And he arose, and rebuked the wind, and said unto the sea, Peace, be still. And the wind ceased, and there was a great calm.'" She repeated the words from Mark's gospel over and over again while the flood waters rose higher and higher, lapping at her feet and ankles and creeping up to her knees. She shivered uncontrollably in the icy water. With all the strength she had, she pulled herself higher into the tree.

The sounds of groaning, breaking, shattering wood rode on the tide of the storm. Water ran over and around her, threatening to pull her into its deadly flow.

Exhausted, she clamped her body around the trunk with her last bit of strength. Riding on the top of the flood she spotted broken beams and patches of wood. *The bridge was gone. Help, God.*

If Noah survived forty days of nonstop rain, she could survive this. This flood wouldn't last nearly that long. God had promised.

Thoughts of Noah didn't make Mary Anne any warmer. God would never again destroy the earth with a flood, but people died in flood waters every year. Her life could end here, tonight.

Minutes felt like hours and hours felt like days. Mary Anne clung to the branch, repeated Bible verses embedded in her mind, and waited for the water to pass. After a time, she realized that rain splashed her body and not river water.

If she had stayed in New York and gone to the police after her father's death, she wouldn't be clinging to a tree during a flood. She wouldn't have been crossing the bridge into Maple Notch on that fateful Thursday night seven months ago.

If she hadn't crossed the bridge, she wouldn't have run into Wallace's car, and she couldn't imagine life without him.

If she had a life.

What a mess.

"Mary Anne?" A voice sliced through the rain and darkness.

"Wallace?" She peered through the darkness below her but couldn't see him.

"Mary Anne?" He sounded a little closer.

She slumped in relief. "Wallace!"

"Mary Anne!"

They continued their flood-induced version of hide-and-seek until Wallace sloshed through the water at her feet.

He looked up into the tree, his glasses knocked askew, joy written on his face. "I love you, Mary Anne Lamont!"

"I love you, Wallace Tuttle!" she yelled back.

With a grin defying the gravity of the situation, he locked his arms over the bottom limb and climbed until he joined her midway up the trunk. "Help is coming."

Mary Anne's heart melted. The silly man had braved water and destruction to join her in her tree perch. "Can't we climb down?"

He shook his head. "It's not safe for man nor beast down there. I don't want to put you in any further danger."

"Then why did you come?"

"I figured, if I couldn't protect you from the flood, I could at least face it with you."

This man meant what he said. The rain flattened his thick brown hair against his forehead, giving her a glimpse into what he would look like if he went bald. Still a handsome man, she decided.

She didn't have time for any further thoughts as he leaned closer, closer, and claimed her lips in a kiss.

Wallace cherished every minute he spent with Mary Anne in the tree. Mary Anne shared details he had never before known about her. Now that she had torn the lid off her past, all her hidden dreams escaped in an outpouring of memories big and small.

She demanded the same of him. "What about you, Wallace? Do you want to write more books?"

"I thought I did. That's what I told my family I wanted to do, and they let me pursue my dream."

"And now you've written a book. I can't wait to see it."

Wallace hoped the editor felt the same way. "I think I had to write *this* book, about our birds."

"Those baby raccoons are so much fun, you should write a book about them, too."

He shrugged, his shoulder bumping hers. "Maybe. But the question is what God wants for me. I'll always be involved with the Audubon Society, but I don't know about more books. Not yet."

With Mary Anne in his arms, Wallace felt strangely warm. On a night of the impossible and improbable, one thing had yet to be uttered.

"There is one thing I know for sure about the rest of my life."

"Oh? What is that?"

"Who I want to spend it with. *You*. As soon as we put this mess behind us, I'm going to ask you to marry me. So you need to decide if a city girl like you wants to spend the rest of her life with me, here in Maple Notch."

"I don't need time." Mary Anne smiled so sweetly that he kissed her again.

The cold deepened, and they drew together for warmth. "They'll find us soon." Wallace hoped that was true. He had left everyone behind in the cave. They talked to keep themselves awake, fearful of falling if they went to sleep.

Chill seeped into their bones and pried Wallace's tight grip away from the tree trunk. In the deepest part of the night, welcome flashlights flickered beneath them. "We'll get you out of there as fast as we can." Wallace could see Howard's face illuminated by the light. "We've got ladders here."

Wallace climbed onto the ladder first, pausing after he descended a couple of steps. "Come ahead, Mary Anne. I've got you." They descended the ladder rungs in tandem, her inside the sheltering reach of his arms as if she was made to fit there. Once on the ground, their pastor draped blankets around them and guided them to a high spot where they could dry out by a fire.

Later, after they made it back to the seminary, Aunt Flo filled them with as much tea as they could swallow and enough warm soup to bring their body temperatures back up to normal. Wallace asked to speak with the constable. "Did they escape?"

From their long conversation, Wallace knew Mary Anne feared retribution from DiNapoli's gang almost more than the flood waters.

Smith looked at Gerard, who answered. "They weren't as lucky as you. They were so busy trying to get the hooch out of the hiding place they didn't even notice the river was rising until it was too late."

"They…drowned?"

This time Gerard looked to Smith for answers. "We found two bodies downstream. We'll need you to identify them for us, Miss Lamont, to confirm they were the men who were in the car with you."

"And the whiskey?" Wallace asked.

"Let's just say a whole lot of fish downstream are breaking the eighteenth amendment tonight." Smith flashed a rare smile.

All that profit, washed downstream. Smith brought up the thorny problem that remained. "We've been building a case against DiNapoli for some time. We can't bring him to court for the whiskey, since all the evidence washed away. And the man who killed your father is dead. From what you told us, DiNapoli is implicated in the conspiracy to commit murder. We need your testimony."

Wallace held his breath, but Mary Anne didn't hesitate. "I'm tired of hiding. I'll do whatever it takes to bring that snake to justice." She flicked a glance at her hands, then raised her eyes to meet Smith's. "And I'll turn what's left of the money over to the government. I'm tired of all the problems that came with it."

Smith managed a smile at that statement. "That's not necessary. You can keep it, or give it all to the real St. Ignatius's Children's Fund, if you want to."

"Daddy would like that."

Six months later

"Your mother would have been very proud of you, I'm sure." Aunt Flo's hands fluttered at Mary Anne's back, adjusting the tulle veil that came with the gown Mama had worn at her wedding. "What a beautiful dress. The way the lace covers the pleats on the chiffon makes you look feminine and dainty." She laughed. "Although we both know how very independent you are. You are a strong, proud woman. My mother would have approved."

Mary Anne felt humbled at the ultimate compliment from Florence Tuttle, comparison to her beloved mother and founder of the Maple Notch Female Seminary, Clara Farley Tuttle.

"Enough of that." Clarinda lightly scolded her aunt. "What's important is that she's the right woman for our Wallace. We are glad to have her join our family." She tweaked the veil around Mary Anne's face, stroking the curl that folded over her temples and swept back to her ears.

Mary Anne was the only non-Tuttle in the wedding party. Clarinda was her matron of honor, while Winnie was a junior bridesmaid and little Betty was her flower girl. All the women were dressed in blue satin with a hint of sequins around a sweetheart neckline.

In keeping with the Tuttle family's tradition of forward thinking for women, Mary Anne had asked Aunt Flo to give her away. After a school year of serving as Mary Anne's employer, teacher and mentor, Aunt Flo seemed the most suited to the role.

Clarinda and Winnie carried a single yellow tulip apiece.

Azalea petals like the ones from the clusters Mary Anne carried filled little Betty's basket. Red tulips rounded out the bridal bouquet.

"It's time." The pastor's wife appeared in the doorway. The bridal party strolled down the hall, arm in arm, to the opening chords of the Bridal Chorus.

Winnie disappeared through the doors, followed by little Betty, then Clarinda. Mary Anne went last, accompanied by Aunt Flo.

When she turned the corner to the sanctuary, Wallace filled her vision. He filled her future.

From this day forward until death do us part.

With the wedding behind them, the rest of their lives opened before them, and Wallace knew where he wanted to start.

On their way out of Maple Notch, heading to nearby Stowe for a honeymoon, Wallace drove the Victoria coupe in the direction of the Bumblebee River.

"Isn't Stowe in the other direction?" Mary Anne looked out the window in confusion.

"We have a stop to make first." Wallace parked a few feet before the Road Closed sign near the bank of the river that warned traffic to stay away until the bridge reconstruction was complete.

"What are we doing here?" Mary Anne hadn't come this near the river since they had spent the night in the tree last November.

"Come and see." Wallace couldn't stop smiling. His face would hurt tomorrow from the daylong stretch on his features. "You know they're rebuilding the bridge into a two-lane road. Not as romantic as the old bridge, but it will be safer." He helped Mary Anne out of the car and led her past the sign.

Already a road marker waited at the side of the bridge.

Mary Anne scanned the words, which told how this was the site of one of Vermont's most historic covered bridges, a few mentions of its role in local history as well as its status as the community's courting bridge. "That's lovely."

"That's not why I brought you here." Wallace beckoned her forward. "Come onto the bridge with me."

She placed her hand in his, with complete trust, and Wallace led her to a pile of rescued planks, intended for reuse. "It's time we christen the new bridge, don't you think?" His lips found hers, and he prayed generations of Tuttles yet to come could enjoy the old tradition.

When he at last relinquished her lips, he pulled a Swiss army knife from his pants pocket. "Now we need to add our initials, to make it official." He carved deep into the wood, the double-V shape that formed the W, and added the T. He handed her the knife. "Your turn."

Mary Anne's first stroke was light, but then she increased the pressure. The *M* reversed the strokes for a *W*. He hadn't noticed that before. *A. L.* "Although officially it's *T,* now." Mary Anne leaned forward, holding on to the lapels of his suit jacket.

"This isn't a kissing bridge," Wallace said.

Mary Anne brought her lips to his. "Yes, it is. It's the bridge of dreams, where our deepest desires come true."

* * * * *

Author's Note

The flood described in Hidden Dreams *is based on the flood in November 1927, the worst flood in Vermont history. Between late evening of November 2 and late morning on November 4, 8.71 inches of rain fell. Eighty-five people lost their lives. Another nine thousand became homeless. Over 1,200 bridges were demolished.*

REQUEST YOUR FREE BOOKS!

2 FREE INSPIRATIONAL NOVELS
PLUS 2
FREE
MYSTERY GIFTS

Love Inspired®

LIDIR13R

REQUEST YOUR FREE BOOKS!

2 FREE RIVETING INSPIRATIONAL NOVELS PLUS 2 FREE MYSTERY GIFTS

Love Inspired®
SUSPENSE

YES! Please send me 2 FREE Love Inspired® Suspense novels and my 2 FREE mystery gifts (gifts are worth about $10). After receiving them, if I don't wish to receive any more books, I can return the shipping statement marked "cancel." If I don't cancel, I will receive 4 brand-new novels every month and be billed just $4.74 per book in the U.S. or $5.24 per book in Canada. That's a savings of at least 21% off the cover price. It's quite a bargain! Shipping and handling is just 50¢ per book in the U.S. and 75¢ per book in Canada.* I understand that accepting the 2 free books and gifts places me under no obligation to buy anything. I can always return a shipment and cancel at any time. Even if I never buy another book, the two free books and gifts are mine to keep forever.

123/323 IDN F5AN

Name _____ (PLEASE PRINT) _____

Address _____ Apt. # _____

City _____ State/Prov. _____ Zip/Postal Code _____

Signature (if under 18, a parent or guardian must sign)

Mail to the Harlequin® Reader Service:
IN U.S.A.: P.O. Box 1867, Buffalo, NY 14240-1867
IN CANADA: P.O. Box 609, Fort Erie, Ontario L2A 5X3

**Are you a current subscriber to Love Inspired Suspense books and want to receive the larger-print edition?
Call 1-800-873-8635 or visit www.ReaderService.com.**

* Terms and prices subject to change without notice. Prices do not include applicable taxes. Sales tax applicable in N.Y. Canadian residents will be charged applicable taxes. Offer not valid in Quebec. This offer is limited to one order per household. Not valid for current subscribers to Love Inspired Suspense books. All orders subject to credit approval. Credit or debit balances in a customer's account(s) may be offset by any other outstanding balance owed by or to the customer. Please allow 4 to 6 weeks for delivery. Offer available while quantities last.

Your Privacy—The Harlequin® Reader Service is committed to protecting your privacy. Our Privacy Policy is available online at www.ReaderService.com or upon request from the Harlequin Reader Service.
We make a portion of our mailing list available to reputable third parties that offer products we believe may interest you. If you prefer that we not exchange your name with third parties, or if you wish to clarify or modify your communication preferences, please visit us at www.ReaderService.com/consumerchoice or write to us at Harlequin Reader Service Preference Service, P.O. Box 9062, Buffalo, NY 14269. Include your complete name and address.

LISDIR13R

REQUEST YOUR FREE BOOKS!

2 FREE INSPIRATIONAL NOVELS
PLUS 2
FREE
MYSTERY GIFTS

Love Inspired.
HISTORICAL
INSPIRATIONAL HISTORICAL ROMANCE

YES! Please send me 2 FREE Love Inspired® Historical novels and my 2 FREE mystery gifts (gifts are worth about $10). After receiving them, if I don't wish to receive any more books, I can return the shipping statement marked "cancel." If I don't cancel, I will receive 4 brand-new novels every month and be billed just $4.74 per book in the U.S. or $5.24 per book in Canada. That's a savings of at least 21% off the cover price. It's quite a bargain! Shipping and handling is just 50¢ per book in the U.S. and 75¢ per book in Canada.* I understand that accepting the 2 free books and gifts places me under no obligation to buy anything. I can always return a shipment and cancel at any time. Even if I never buy another book, the two free books and gifts are mine to keep forever.

102/302 IDN F5CY

Name	(PLEASE PRINT)	
Address		Apt. #
City	State/Prov.	Zip/Postal Code

Signature (if under 18, a parent or guardian must sign)

Mail to the Harlequin® Reader Service:
IN U.S.A.: P.O. Box 1867, Buffalo, NY 14240-1867
IN CANADA: P.O. Box 609, Fort Erie, Ontario L2A 5X3

Want to try two free books from another series?
Call 1-800-873-8635 or visit www.ReaderService.com.

* Terms and prices subject to change without notice. Prices do not include applicable taxes. Sales tax applicable in N.Y. Canadian residents will be charged applicable taxes. Offer not valid in Quebec. This offer is limited to one order per household. Not valid for current subscribers to Love Inspired Historical books. All orders subject to credit approval. Credit or debit balances in a customer's account(s) may be offset by any other outstanding balance owed by or to the customer. Please allow 4 to 6 weeks for delivery. Offer available while quantities last.

LIHDIR13R

SPECIAL EXCERPT FROM

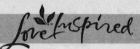

What happens when opposites attract?

Read on for a sneak peek at
SEASIDE BLESSINGS by Irene Hannon,
available June 2013 from Love Inspired.

Clint Nolan padded barefoot toward the front of the house as the doorbell gave an impatient peal. After spending the past hour fighting a stubborn tree root on the nature trail at The Point, he wanted food, not visitors.

Forcibly changing his scowl to the semblance of a smile, he unlocked the door, pulled it open—and froze.

It was her.

Miss Reckless-Driver. Kristen Andrews.

And she didn't look any too happy to see him.

His smile morphed back to a scowl.

Several seconds of silence ticked by.

Finally he spoke. "Can I help you?" The question came out cool and clipped.

She cleared her throat. "I, uh, got your address from the town's bulletin board. Genevieve at the Orchid recommended your place when I, uh, ate dinner there."

Since he'd arrived in town almost three years ago, the sisters at the Orchid had been lamenting his single state. Especially Genevieve.

But the Orchid Café matchmaker was wasting her time. The inn's concierge wasn't the woman for him. No way. Nohow.

And Kristen herself seemed to agree.

"I doubt you'd be interested. It's on the *rustic* side," he said.

LIEXP7818

spark of indignation sprang to life in her eyes, and her chin ose in a defiant tilt.

Uh-oh. Wrong move.

"Depends on what you mean by rustic. Are you telling me doesn't have indoor plumbing?"

He folded his arms across his chest. "It has a full bath and compact kitchen. Very compact."

"How many bedrooms?"

"Two. Plus living room and breakfast nook."

"It's furnished, correct?"

"With the basics."

"I'd like to see it."

Okay. She was no airhead, even if she did spend her days rranging cushy excursions and making dinner reservations or rich hotel guests. But there was an undeniable spark of ntelligence—and spunk—in her eyes. She might be uncomortable around him, but she hadn't liked the implication of is rustic comment one little bit and she was going to make im pay for it. One way or another…

Will Clint and Kristen ever see eye to eye?

Don't miss SEASIDE BLESSINGS by Irene Hannon, on sale June 2013 wherever Love Inspired books are sold!

♡

HEARTSONG
PRESENTS

Look out for 4 new
Heartsong Presents books next month!

**Every month 4 inspiring faith-filled
romances will be available in stores.**

These contemporary and historical Christian
romances emphasize God's role in every
relationship and reinforce the importance of
faith, hope and love.